MW01595133

THE MIDGARD INSTITUTE
OF SCIENCE FICTION & FANTASY LITERATURE PRESENTS:

THE BIZARCHIVES
Weird Tales of Monsters, Magic, and Machines

Volume 2

December 2021

Published in 2021:
The Bizarchives
TheBizarchives.com

Printed in the United States of America.

Cover Art: Dunelord's Dreaming by Donald Kent
Interior Art by Donald Kent
Layout: Michael Sagginario

Table of Contents

Letter to Our Readers

Dear readers,

I wanted to open this issue with something candid. A direct message from us to you. Because, mostly in the world of literature and film, the relationship between creator and viewer is detached. In mainstream media -- whether it be Hollywood, videogames, or the books written by big publisher's darlings -- there's an ivory tower situation, where multi-million dollar corporations view people only through sales data and marketing analytics.

They don't know us, they don't talk to us, nor do they care what we have to say. So as a result they pump out increasingly mediocre crap with the aim of mass appeal. One-size-fits-all soulless garbage meant to dazzle with special effects and then be discarded like a cheeseburger wrapper. The viewer is sucked into an endless consumer cycle, never being satiated.

Then on top of all of it they shoehorn in the newest political narrative in order to pander and subvert, mocking us in the process. I can't tell you how many times I've put down a book or left a movie theater not only feeling disappointed but insulted. Our favorite stories, heroes, and settings are meaningful to us. They were there when we wanted to escape from dark times, they inspired us, and they gave us strength when we needed it.

And most importantly, many of these stories were shared with us by our parents and grandparents. And we share them with our children today. It's not just make believe fables. These are storytelling traditions. In ancient times, they told about Beowulf, Odysseus, and King Arthur. In today's times, we tell about Conan and Samwise Gamgee.

So instead of just posting on social media how disgruntled I was about my favorite stories being ruined, I decided to create new ones. Someone told me in a comment section once "Don't like it? Make your own." So I did. And in a few days I had a whole folder of submissions from talented writers who had the same vision that I did.

With your help and support, we smashed our milestones out of the atmosphere, tripling our yearly sales goal in the first month. I started this project with the little bit of money I put aside from my pandemic stimulus checks. Now, thanks to all you, The Bizarchives is rapidly transforming into a legitimate publishing operation. Writers who have never been given a chance can now see their names in print. You gave them a chance to fulfill their dream.

Therefore, as a bonus for all your support, we've collaborated with the mighty Donald Kent from American Zarathustra for an exclusive issue containing full interior art. Authors, artists and readers all coming together to breathe life into what we love: Weird Fiction.

I want to take a few moments to personally thank you, the readers, for your participation in The Bizarchives' success.

The Silver Key
by Dave Martel

The conceptualization of time itself has decayed. It has become inconceivable. You have no means of measuring how long you've haunted The Bizarchives and its countless wonders. One after another, you pull tomes from their perches and feverishly read them to their completion with no cognizance of day, week, or year. There is neither sun nor moonlight here. Only the dancing hues of numerous artefacts and oddities and a bottomless looming darkness above you. But never have you been stricken with fear or homesickness. Nor have you stopped to consider anything beyond satiating your newfound hunger for this knowledge.

"Here," the voice of the mysterious man startles you. You turn to see in his palms a peculiar obsidian box engraved with oblong eyes and tentacles that blink and writhe as if they were living. Within the box a silken lining of off-green. Nested in the box lies a tarnished silver key. Queer but ornate in design. The haft twists and swirls with an ophidian quality. The butt an intriguing but indiscernible mashing of symbols into a nimbus-like shape.

1

"What is this?" you ask with obsessive gaze.

The man smirks, "This is our most cherished artefact. It unlocks a gateway to the Mysterium, the dreamsea. A realm of imagination and wonder."

You reach into the box and grip the key with your fingers. Cool to the touch but not abnormal. You lift it to your eyes for intimate inspection.

"How did you get this?" you inquire

"Long ago, there was a man of incredible brilliance. He envisioned worlds of great wonder and told tales of terrible beings. Through his prose he gave others a glimpse into the dreamsea. In life he was the silver key. Now we hold but a manifestation of it. It was a gift from him to us," he explains

You ponder for a moment and reply, "But how can there be a realm of dreams when dreams aren't real?"

The man pulls back his hood to reveal his flowing silver hair as it falls down the back of his robes. "Real. What is real? Allow me to ask you this. In your world there are deep ocean trenches filled with creatures never seen by the human eye. Ask the common people to draw an image of one of these creatures and they will be unable to do so. It might as well not exist. Then ask them to draw a dragon and you will then have a pile of sketches depicting winged reptiles breathing fire. Which is more real? The unknown creature of material quality or the completely conceptualized immaterial creature?"

He continues, "This is why you're here. Why you've sought this place. In your world they have scoffed at the imaginative. Every child has their inspiration methodically cut from their souls as if it were a cancerous growth, leaving a population of walking corpses with no hope nor vision.

"You've built a prison around yourselves where the

only truth is material and the only accepted thoughts are increasingly meaningless abstractions. Your world has been sterilized by science. And to fill the void, they participate in more and more masochism. They have no heroes, no true innovations and no forward-thrusting spirit. Stagnant insectoids numbing their intellects with narcotics and screens. But as long as this key exists, those who desire it may remember how to dream."

You lift the key into the air as if to plunge it into some phantom lock. A phantasmal force guides your motions without your consent. Where you imagine the key should be inserted, an ethereal ripple travels outward with a humming wobble sound. From the point of the key, shimmering gold traces shoot out and rapidly cast the outline of a large arched door. Within moments, the outline fills itself with the translucent visage of a wondrous gateway. A shining golden door adorned with a blinding array of glitter and gemstones. Engraved upon its front, masterful depictions of mythic creatures and stunning constellations.

As the ripple dissipates, the door manifests fully into a semi-material form still maintaining a ghost-like lucidity. An illuminating bluish mist slowly obscures your surroundings. A crank of the key cuts loose an echoing click. By its own volition, the door heavily swings awide.

Your eyes are forced shut by a blinding sheen as what lies behind the door is revealed. You are enchanted by a strong breeze that briskly howls into the room. It refreshes you, yet it has no discernable coolness or warmth. It blows, yet your hair and clothes remain still. You experience its delightful sensations, yet no effect can be observed. It is both real and unreal. Surreal perhaps. As your eyes adjust what unfurls before you as you stand at the threshold is a sight undreamed of. Stimulating so intensely that tears of sadness cascade to smiling lips. Laughter, fear, grief all liberate themselves at once for a schizophrenic cacophony of saccharine primality.

Beyond the door, an immeasurable landscape passes beneath you as if you were surveying a wondrous planetscape from atop a flying carpet. Herculean mountain ranges with crystalline snow tops. Puffs of icy powder trail from shards of rock faces as they dislodge and tumble. The peaks circled by majestic winged beasts unleashing echoing shrieks from their long fearsome beaks. Beyond the mountains, a vast feature-less chasm of volcanic rock. Melting boulders helplessly drift down crawling rivers of lava, far larger than any earthbound river and too numerous to count. From the jagged cliff edges of obsidian glass, the molten orange oozes and plummets to the chasm depths. Only a distant orange glow is visible beneath the dense toxic fog of sulphuric steam. Rumbling geysers burp forth poisonous gas and tectonic innards.

The black rock morphs into lush grasslands where magnificent docile creatures graze. Thick tufts of orange-brown shag dangle from their hides as they lean to their back legs using long articulating fingers to grasp pearlescent fruits from the tops of towering fungi. The earth quakes as the gargantuan grazers set their massive front limbs back onto the ground. In the distance upon sandy plateaus stand marvelous palaces of silver and ivory. Stained glass dome roofs display heroic ballads of ages yet to come and never were. Pristine marble corridors haunted only by the whistling whisper of gentle wind. A lavish royal chamber holding an empty throne with no heir nor claimant in sight. From the castle a blanketing, unending forest. Raw and primordial. Powerful trees, millennia old shrouding all beneath in darkness. Slithering carnivorous vines seeking curious mammalian bipeds to feast. Thousands of gangly simian swingers travel from branch to branch among the vast forest canopy like a pod of dolphins leaping through an ocean of leafy green.

Finally, the world stops to give you a picturesque view of a serene sapphire seascape. A waning evening sun sinks behind the horizon. The waters begin to disturb as your ears are assaulted by a thunderous disjointed groan. The sun begins to bleed an eerie purple essence into its sphere casting a chthonic aura. The clouds blacken with toiling hate as they swirl typhonically. Your heart beats faster as the trumpeting groan rattles the earth and distorts into a ghastly choir of nightmarish pitch.

The water roils as thousands of eelish appendages emerge from the waves in a pulsing, formless mass. Thousands of deranged voices pollute your mind. All spitting hateful curses in thousands of long-dead tongues. The maddening crescendo comes to a sudden silence as two titanic glowing red eyes appear just beneath the surface. Their stare punctures their way into the furthest depths of your consciousness, drinking your memories and tasting your fears. You feel as though you are being summoned into their abyssal glow. You want to just let go and tumble headfirst into the writhing mass and be subsumed by this terrible æonic being. You offer your mind as its chalice to relish in the nectar of your sanity.

SLAM the door swings shut, sending you to your back. The outlines rapidly retract as the glitter and gold of the wondrous door fade. The entire door soon vanishes, and the key clangs onto the floor, no longer being suspended. Your senses return as you desperately try to regain your breath.

"Wh..what was that?" you pant

The robed man pulls you to your feet. "The man from whom this key manifested wielded great power. Although, in life, only those who saw his brilliance could see. He had prophetic insight into your world and the consequences of its follies, though many today curse him for it. He used his sight into the dreamsea to inspire countless souls to reach into it themselves. Many of the tomes you read here were inspired by his magnificent imaginative capacity. He will never be named among those whom your world considers as genius. But he belongs there."

"So what was that monster?" you ask

"You see. The master of the silver key wanted more than anything to help men dream again. But his legacy was reaching deep into man's most primal emotion. Fear. And he left behind not dreams of mystical worlds but unforgettable nightmares that will haunt men until they are inevitably swallowed by the hungering void," he says as points to your pocket.

You reach into your pocket and pull out a tarnished silver key. An exact duplicate of the key you previously used. You hold it out in your palm and look upon its features.

"You experienced the magic of the dreamsea, and now you know that it is indeed real. Whenever one peers into its wonder and its terror they can never lose its inspiration. So they then have the key to share with others. And eventually man will remember what it is to be inspired. And on that day they will once again dream of heroes and innovations. They will build great marvels and perform great feats. It all starts with this key," the keeper says as he scoops up the first key from the floor and carefully places it into the box.

"And who was the master of the silver key? What was his name?" You ask

The wizard pulls his hood back over his head and a wide smirk cuts across his face.

"Howard. His name was Howard Phillips Lovecraft."

The Bizarchives

The Dune Lord's Dreaming
by MS Jones

"We don't eat, we don't sleep and we don't bleed, but we don't come cheap," I say, standing to my full height and puffing out my chest like a good soldier. I believe that it's important to make a professional impression, even if I am already dead.

Many of the tavern's customers move away when they see a revenant among them; a few come closer to get a better look at the living dead man. It brings me no pride to know that I am now the subject of many of the whispered conversations in the tavern.

"Gold will not be a problem," the ochre-skinned merchant replies, looking me up and down and checking me out like a camel at market. He is dressed in rich silks and dripping in jewellery, so there is no doubt of his affluence.

"My master has gold, much gold, and he will have much more once we deliver our cargo safely to Tarobane. That is

9

why he wants *you*, my friend." He takes a step towards me and slaps me on the arm twice, rattling my armour and raising a cloud of dust which sets him coughing.

"Ten thousand coins will buy you my full company for the duration of the voyage," I say, fixing him with my gaze, looking to cow him with my hideous visage and cut short the negotiations. My desiccated skin, the colour of decay pulled taught over an almost-visible skull is not pleasant to look at up close, I am told.

"Unacceptable!" He spits, clearly unimpressed by the stare of living death. "That's almost a quarter of our profits."

"Better three-quarters of the profit of a full cargo than all the profit from none," I reason and turn my back on him and walk towards the door. I know his type well; his master knows my price and is prepared to pay it; otherwise, we would not be having this conversation. He's just trying to hold out and get a cut for himself. My men and I are worth double that price, and he knows it, too.

"The road through the desert is perilous," I remind him. "There are sand walkers, dust drakes, lightning hawks. Lots of dangers lie between here and the markets of Tarobane, never mind the sand storms. But if you would rather employ someone else, there is an open market for caravan guards here in Lubach. Be my guest."

"It is too much. My master..." He comes running after me as I knew he would.

"Your master sent you to find the best guards for your caravan, and you have: you have found me. Now, are you prepared to pay my price or not?"

"Eight thousand." He is stone-faced in negotiation, but I am made of stone.

"Eleven. If that is too much then go tell your master that I have heard that Simbul the Stranger's crew will be back to full strength in a couple of weeks, and he'll be looking for a contract. They lost only half of their number and most of their last cargo getting here. Or maybe you can form your own gang from the dregs in the taverns. There are plenty of men here who will be happy to take your coin - although I'm not sure how many of them will stand their ground to defend you against the sand walkers when they come nor how many will live to see the white towers of Tarobane, but perhaps their price will be *acceptable*."

"My friend, I do not doubt your prowess, but ten thousand coins is too great a price even for a renowned company such as yours."

"It's eleven thousand now, or have you forgotten the extra thousand for wasting my time?"

"What do the dead need with so many coins?" He throws out his arms in desperation and asks the sky. He doesn't need to know the answer, but we need it as much as any warm-blood. The blood spice we crave does not come cheap.

"Take your time," I say. "I'm sure Tarobane's winter will wait for your wool, although I have heard that Turman Berq is leaving Ransol soon with his own cargo. Maybe the Tarobani won't have to wait for their undergarments while you waste your time wondering about things that don't concern you." Any caravan making it across the desert with goods from Lubach's ports would command a high price in Tarobane, but the first to arrive would always have a bonanza.

"You are truly a heartless devil, captain. Nine thousand and I'm slitting my own throat."

"Twelve, and I'll be happy to slit it for you." My grey-lipped grin leaves my intentions ambiguous.

"The space saved on your camels' backs by not having to bring food and drink for my men will more than make up for our cost, any shrewd merchant would know that." It was true, one camel load of wine and metalwork from the isles leaving from Lubach would make enough profit for a modest man's lifetime in the markets of Tarobane. Investing that wisely in silks and spices could make ten times that on the return journey. This man's bickering over the price of getting there safely to collect his treasure irritates me.

"I do not have the funds for twelve thousand. Ten thousand is all my master provided."

"Then sell a camel or two. It's twelve thousand, or you wait for a willing gang of warmbloods and you take your chances with them. Besides, you'll probably feel safer with your own kind. Everybody wins.

"Now if you don't mind, I have a serious merchant to see about a contract to guard his caravan. If I come back here, the price will have risen to fifteen thousand."

Every one of the merchant caravans leaving Lubach to go to Tarobane want me and my men to protect them, so we can afford to be choosy about our contracts. Ten thousand is the minimum for the trip, but most are prepared to offer more to guarantee our services. We are *The Bloodthirsters*, the most notorious caravanserai on the Old Salt Road - we have never reneged on a contract and never lost a cargo to the sand walkers yet. I say men in the loosest sense; we are all revenants: the living dead. Dust devils, some call us, or sand walkers if they are feeling less generous.

We died, all of us, centuries ago, along with the empire that we served, Sirrissa, may its name be cursed for ten thousand eternities as we are. What was once a fertile continent was turned into a dust bowl as the empire crumbled at the whim of the dark thaumaturgy of some forgotten gods.

Sirrissa may have fallen to dust, but many of its inhabitants fared even worse. Torn between the obligation of the enchanted bonds of servitude to their god-emperor and the eldritch magics that devastated the empire, death could not take them completely.

Once the war was over, they crawled from the sands. Many were mindless creatures following the catastrophe, and they became the feral sand walkers, wandering the desert attacking anyone they found. A few of us were lucky (or doubly cursed), and we retained some shards of intellect. We became revenants, denied the grave and denied true life. Over the years we found others like ourselves and found a common purpose and a common desire, the blood spice.

Not only did Sirrissa's collapse curse its inhabitants and damn the desert, it also left two civilisations stranded at its extremities. The Dragon Spine Mountains to the west and the boiling sea to the east of the shattered peninsula were all but impassable, and that made the desert road, the Old Salt Road, the only viable trade route for any sizable cargo. As long as the rich have gold enough to indulge their frivolities, they will find a way to get what they want, so a caravan route sprang up across the desert to bring luxuries from one city to the other.

Tough, unyielding and already dead, we make ideal soldiers. Protecting the caravans became a way for us to earn the money required to pay for the blood spice.

My men wait outside town. There's no need for them to pay the toll to enter the city; there's nothing they need in Lubach. Only Tarobane holds any desire for us.

Black Raydon stands sentry. He's a statue clothed in the desert's colours; an unwary man might not see him standing there until he was almost upon him. The only movement is the fluttering of his ragged clothing in the wind along with the tattered pennant on the end of his spear. His ebony eyes fix me as I pass, but he makes no challenge.

There are currently thirty-one men in the company, all dead like me. We are not prejudiced, but the living cannot stand our company for long. Maybe it's the silence. Our mummified, grey-black flesh has been desiccated beneath the sands and then tanned to impregnable leather in the sun of the Sirrissan desert, so it couldn't be the smell.

Several of my men bear wounds that will never heal - Kelf has only one arm, but he can strap a shield to the remaining stump, and he wields his spear as well as any of the company, so we keep him. Cratha the Silent lost his jawbone and most of his face to a wolf pack over a century ago, but he was never a great talker; none of us are. All our talking is done, all our thinking is over, all our desires are fled - except for the blood spice, our own special vice that can only be found in Tarobane's fleshpots. That is why we work.

"So?" Rannar, my lieutenant, asks. "Do we have a contract, or do we have to go back penniless?"

"We have a contract. The fat fool will be here tomorrow for my mark, and we can head back."

"Good. I will tell the men."

14

Three weeks into the journey and we are approaching the ruined caravanserai the merchants call Midway. So far we've been lucky, and we have seen little trouble on the road. The merchants are already whispering that we have taken their money for nothing, that the dangers of the desert were exaggerated, and that we have played them for fools. They should be thankful that their money has bought them so much peace.

Our bows have kept the lightning birds at bay, and Crow-eye, our best scout, spotted a giant sun scorpion's nest close to the road a couple of days ago, and we were able to avoid it. Maybe we should have roused it instead and slaughtered the ferocious beast under the merchants' noses to show the fools what their coin was buying.

As sunset approaches, we traipse silently along what might once have been a major road, but which is now barely a track, through a ruined gateway into a scattered plain of ruins. Judging by the spread of the broken buildings, the Midway caravanserai was once a great city. The foundations of a broken bridge hang over a void where a river once ran.

Unbidden, the picture of the place as a bustling port full of life, like Lubach already weeks behind us, fills my mind. I imagine merchants selling fresh fish from their forgotten river alongside robed merchants offering the luxurious commodities from both ends of the Old Salt Road to a prosperous, happy citizenry. Then the wind blows a tumbleweed across my field of vision which drags the memory with it.

Whatever this place had been, it is now nothing but an empty shell. The river is long-gone, and only one spring remains, which has to be unblocked anew by each caravan that visits (no warmblood would dare stay here to keep the place serviceable).

The old city may have fallen into ruin, but its debris provides some shelter for the warmbloods. My men couldn't care less, but it is still a pleasing sight as it marks the halfway point of our journey to Tarobane and the blood spice.

The road south has taken us in a wide westerly arc to avoid the worst corruption of Sirrissa, the capital of the fallen empire which still taints the desert. I can always feel it, the epicentre of the forgotten catastrophe calling to me. Tomorrow we will start heading south-east, away from its lure.

"Tommin, get the spring ready for our guests."

"Yes sir," he replies. The flag that normally marks the spring lies in the sand almost hidden, but the boy knows where to find it and starts digging. It is funny that I still think of him as a boy; he was one when he died, a drummer looking for excitement in the ranks he says; now he is several hundred years old but frozen in a boy's frame.

"A storm is coming," I say to Rannar. I feel it on my skin, one of the few things I can still feel. "The tents will be useless - better to shelter in the ruins," I tell the merchants.

"Gather your beasts in the old town square." I point to a place where cracked marble flagstones are still visible beneath the sand and the scrub grass and the walls remain high and sturdy in several places. The camels are restless and resent being moved. It might just be the storm, but their snorting and pissing are spreading their worry to the warmbloods.

"Help them secure the beasts," I shout to Cratha over the wind. He picks up several of the reins and pulls them together over his shoulder and drags the creatures to the chosen spot. Then he pulls downward, driving them to their knees. The merchants start unloading the camels and pile their precious goods in the centre of the makeshift camp, eyeing us warily in the process.

"We do not steal, and we will not drink your spice wine in the night," Black Raydon says in reply to their worried glances. "We are *The Bloodthirsters*. That is enough."

While they prepare the campfires for the night I go to visit the stelae one more time. I am always drawn to them when we camp in Midway. I stand in their long shadows and look up at their capitals, crossed at an incongruous angle close to the centre of the ruins, thrusting from the sand like leaping whales, frozen as they break the water or saved mid-fall by some invisible power. Maybe they were once part of the facade of some monumental building or columns from an aqueduct, I will never know.

While their attitudes are curious, the most intriguing thing about them is the carvings that run around their bases. Someone has been engraving pictographs on their surfaces since before I can remember. The first lines are wind-worn and ancient but still legible; the latest marks are freshly carved and could have been made yesterday.

It is a puzzle to me: a rare distraction in a world where nothing intrigues me anymore. Sometimes the signs repeat for line after line or taper out at the end. Sometimes they are scratched out or written over. They must be the markings of some other company that crosses our path on the Old Salt Road, but what do they represent? Do they tell a story or give a warning in some forgotten tongue, or are they just scribblings, a game devised by bored merchants to pass the time? Somehow, the intricacy and the consistency of the designs insists to me that there is some meaning, some burgeoning message that I will never understand.

The sand walkers' sudden appearance breaks my reverie. They come one by one at first, stumbling out of the sand towards us, but there will be more; there are always more. I don't know how they sense us, but they always know when we are here.

I go to stand at the edge of the camp and survey the desert beyond. The first one shambles past, ignoring me completely - I have nothing it craves. It seeks out the warmbloods huddled together in the centre of the camp. My sword, *Dry Fang*, flashes twilight as it slices its head from its body, severing the chains of magic that kept it in this blighted existence, along with its spinal cord. Decapitation is the quickest way to kill them, but any blow that damages them sufficiently will eventually reduce them to innocuous pieces of shrivelled flesh, although I have seen some dragging their tattered torsos across the sand using only their arms.

The horizon is soon crowded with its kin. They are a storm we must weather with our shields and spears.

"Incoming!" I hear sergeant Ur shouting from behind me without my prompting. He is ever vigilant. "Form up, you maggots."

The men unsling their shields from their backs, huge, sheltering circles bearing our sigil of a single drop of blood etched in black. They link up in practised hands to form the scales of an impenetrable dragon that marches forward to meet the enemy.

Despite the blinding sandstorm hampering us, we are more than a match for them. The first wave barely slows the advance of the shieldwall, but they keep coming in wave after wave, skewering themselves on our spear points until the build-up of lifeless corpses begins to slow our advance.

We are invincible but we are few, and we cannot be everywhere at once. One gets around our cordon and heads for the warmbloods cowering in the camp. It falls on the first camel it comes across. The beast startles to its feet, bleating

18

and bucking in fear, but the sand walker remains locked to its long neck, shaken like a rotten, limbed lamprey.

The beast's mad cries and kicking risk stampeding the other camels until Ur leaves his place behind the line and puts it out of its misery with a swift stab of his trident to the throat which rips the sand walker in two on the backstroke. Ur prefers the trident for precisely this reason, but great strength is needed to avoid getting the weapon stuck in a fallen adversary's corpse.

The camel's blood flows to the sand, where it starts to bubble, then a forest of skeletal arms thrust upward to grab the wounded beast. It disappears under the sand but we are too busy to care about its plight. Sand walkers are crawling out of the sand in the middle of the merchants' camp.

"Form two horns!" I shout, realising the danger. My men obey instinctively, splitting the shield wall into two columns of a dozen men each, angled to funnel the mass of the enemy between them. I hate weakening my forces, but if we don't get to the camp the merchants' lives are forfeit, and there'll be no one left to pay our bill and clear our contract. I will not risk that blemish on our reputation. It would lower our market price.

"Right horn! Get here, now!" I shout. "Left horn! Push those sacks of sand back into the desert where they belong!"

The men of the right horn formation run past me and reform in the square around the terrified merchants. They are doing little to protect themselves even though most of them are better armed than we are. The camels will have to take care of themselves.

The drill is perfected by centuries of practice, and the threat is dealt with efficiently. Our weakness is our low number, especially when fighting on two fronts, which is thankfully rare. The sand walkers usually have no sense of tactics.

However, these attacks seem almost coordinated - as if something is controlling them - a revenant like us? I wonder, or a mad sliver of some lost god's mind risen from the desert?

Then I see him. He stands behind the ranks on a low rise in a sirocco of sand, pale amber-yellow eyes glowing with a cold malevolence appearing to direct the attack with his will alone.

"Hold the line!" I command as I cut a path through the enemy out into the desert to confront him.

He is like us in body, skeletal limbs moving beneath sun-damned skin, but while we dress as soldiers, the remnants of his clothing and the sheer number of gold bracelets, necklaces, anklets and other jewels that adorn his husk suggest that he was once a prince. What would he make of the spice, I wonder. Would he give up his jewels for it?

"Brother, join us," I say in the hope that he understands me but its only reply is a bestial snarl as it turns to face me. Despite how hard I look, I see no intelligence in its eyes. Maybe it was once like us but its life with these beasts has reduced it to one of them, like an alpha wolf, a sand walker able to control the rest of the pack but with no more volition than any of them. I realise with something akin to sadness that there will be no new recruit for *The Bloodthirsters* today.

It understands enough to recognise me as a threat and it starts calling its thralls to it with a rasping cry. I see this as a tactical error since it frees up half of my company to attack them from behind. I take that as another sign that it is nothing more than a feral creature prepared to do whatever it takes for it to survive. I, on the other hand, am ready to sacrifice myself if it will save my men.

The creature doesn't know how to fight. It claws at me

snarling, but I beat it back with *Dry Fang* until it cowers before me, and I dispatch it just like any other mindless sand walker by severing its skull from its spine.

I let its remains, jewels and all, lie where they fall. A gift to the desert.

I head back to the camp where the rest of my men are mopping up the last of the sand walkers. I say nothing of the duel. I know that the merchants would be quick to pillage its corpse like a pack of fat ravens if they saw it.

Will I become like that when I have forgotten everything? Should I feel some kinship to these shambling creatures? We are of the same stock after all. They were killed and reborn beneath the sands, as was I. A waterless baptism for an unwanted second life.

No, I insist to myself, we are different - we might have lost all we were before, but we have recovered some humanity (it is the wrong word I know but I cannot think of a better one).

Back at camp, I see that we have lost a few camels and acquired a lot of piss-stained pants. "Clean yourselves up before we leave," I advise. "You smell worse than the camels. And don't do it in the spring, the next group to pass by here deserve clean water too."

The worst of it is that some of the cargo has to be left behind. The craven merchants expend more time and energy calculating the most lucrative goods, pound for pound and hiding the rest and drawing maps than they ever did trying to defend themselves from the sand walkers.

Our charges are much more vigilant and much more

grateful on the second half of the journey, but once we cross a dry river bed and come in sight of the white towers of Tarobane shimmering like a mirage on the horizon, their talk changes. By the time we pass through the city gates their whispers about how much they have lost in the caravanserai and how overpriced we are, are spoken boldly.

The headman, however, recognises our value and thanks me as he hands me a purse with the agreed sum, and we sign off the contract. The parchment is no longer of any interest to me so I send Tommin to nail it to the back of one of the wooden city gates where honoured contracts are displayed for the benefit of future clients.

With our gains, I pay for the exclusive use of a hostelry for a week. The owner complains as usual but takes our coin, double what he would have charged for living guests. We need peace to appreciate our reward for the journey without the company of warmbloods, so I pay it without question.

The reward is fresh blood spice. Red as rubies and costing ten times their price but worth every single coin. Why does it command such a price? To begin with, it is the pollen from a flower that grows only in a few places high in the Grey Edge Mountains. It spoils almost immediately, and its properties cannot be preserved. Tarobane is one of the few places where it can be delivered and consumed in time before its enchantments fade.

And what does it do that merits such preparation?

For the warmbloods, nothing. While you drink and smoke to dream forgetful dreams, we take the blood spice to remember - our coins buy us our memories.

We revenants came into our lives after death with no recollection of who or what we once were. Our bodies survived without traces of our former lives (perhaps that is what drove the sand walkers mad, who knows). Somehow, I do not waste my time trying to understand the how and why of it; the red spice gives us access to those memories. Its effects are infinite in experience but limited in time.

There is a stoicism to the company as I negotiate with the dealer; mainly because our frozen, dead features can't show the desperation we feel. The price is irrelevant, we want all that he has. A drought of the precious spice always follows our passage. There will be no more here for many months. More than enough time for another return journey to earn the coin we need for the next batch. How many times have we done the journey? How many thousand miles have we walked back and forth under the sun for this brief respite?

The cruel red spice. It lets us relive our memories as if we were there but then it makes us forget them as if they had never been.

Once the landlord has gone and we are alone, I share out the spoils. There is no seniority in the men, so they all get the same: little more than a spoonful for each of them, and I keep the rest for myself, enough to fill a small cup. The men are happy with their share; it is enough for their needs, while I need larger and larger doses for what I want.

While my men sniff their powder from their fingernails, I breathe in the aromas from the cup in front of me like it was rich, red wine that the warmbloods drink, before pouring it down my dry throat in one swift gulp.

As my comrades dance with forgotten wives or play with the memories of children long since turned to dust, all I want to do is remember how to die...

The spice hits almost immediately.

Once I am in its grasp, I have to push aside the silken embraces of the phantasms of my wives and my concubines, ignoring their allures and their entreaties to stay with them - I had been happy here in this imagined anteroom of memory for decades after I first discovered the spice, but now it is merely a distraction from what I need.

I watch dozens of children, my children, crying as I turn my back on them and onward through the infinite layers of the spice's effects. I know that I will find the illusion of contentment wherever I choose to rest, but that is not what I seek. I need to remember how to die.

The red prince seeks me out, and his whirlpool presence spirals me back to another time and another place, which the spice makes real.

I stand in a magnificent throne room of pink marble. My father sits on a silver throne in the centre, surrounded by his thirteen children. Princes and princesses link hands around him: my brothers and sisters.

Seated on his dais, our father orders us to speak the words. We know that he is mad but we know that we must obey him whatever the cost. The crashing of the storms outside makes it clear that it is too late for reason. The enemy is at the gates.

We never knew the full price until it was too late. We were invoking the catastrophe that would destroy Sirrissa, not save it. We were responsible. I am responsible. This is the revelation I am doomed to experience anew for eternity since I forget my guilt each time the effects of the spice wear off.

One of my sisters' spirits, manifest in fingers of white silk, says "Come," in the ancient tongue and drags me back through the sea of spice-consciousness to another past.

She stands next to me in a dusty library, a newly cracked grimoire lies on the table. This where my father has found the words of desolation he thinks will end the war. And there is another spell, a spell of undoing for the curse.

My living stomach churns as I realise that I can see the words of undoing, I can read the words that will end the curse. I frantically repeat them in whispers through my moist-again lips as I commit them to memory.

I know how to use them.

I try to write down the words, but their incipient power consumes both parchment and quill as I scribe them. I know I must get to the city in the sands, Midway, and carve the words onto the temple's columns. I must complete the charm before I forget again. Only sacred stone can hold their power.

There is no time to wait for the men. I tell Ranner my intention; he seems to be the most lucid of the group.

Speed is of the essence: the spice's effects will not last long. The little I have left will spoil long before I make it to Midway.

I buy a camel with the last of our gold; the beast recoils from my undeath, but I will it into accepting me on its back. I insist that the guards open the gate for me, and we ride out into the sandstorm beyond the walls of Tarobane.

Some way through the journey, the camel dies under me. I have ridden it to death, but I am still day's away from Midway. I leave its corpse to the sands and continue on foot, not stopping at all. My ghost siblings' encouragements are fading; the spice's effects are draining with each step I take towards my goal. I sniff the remaining scintilla of spice; it is less potent, but I hope that it is enough to rekindle the dreams until I arrive.

Midway looms out of the desert. The temple columns stand like eager ghosts. My previous inscriptions glow in my spice vision. How long have I been trying? How many times have I forgotten? But it is almost complete. One more phrase, just a few more runes, and the spell of undoing will be complete, and I will die.

I carve the final runes with the tip of my sword. I am eager but the act requires precision, so I must take my time… time I do not have. The fiery words become banal carvings as the spice betrays me once again.

I am alone in the desert with no memory of how I got here. The enigmatic runes of Midway once again capture my attention. The last few look to have been carved very recently. As if my arrival had scared off the carver before he had time to finish.

The Bizarchives

28

Lex and the Odd Village
by Dave Martel

"Ooohh Lucious Lex"

Swoons the voluptuous raven-haired maiden as she dismounts Lex's mighty frame and sinks back into the opposite side of the oblong bronze tub. Hot steam bellows from the soapy water, obscuring the woman's soft but angular features and seductive, almond-shaped blue eyes. She attempts to wipe away some of her running makeup while she slowly wraps her luscious red lips around a freshly lit cigarette and takes a deep puff.

"Now you're what they call a *real man*, Ser Lex," she arouses as she caresses Lex's inner thigh with her soft foot under the water.

"Yes. I am real. Unlike you," Lex responds sternly with an inquisitive glare. He stays motionless with his back leaned against the side of the tub, arms relaxed and partially draped over the tub walls. Beard and stringy brown hair drip with condensation as he slowly shifts into a more upright sitting position. The large bath is dwarfed by the sheer girth of Lex's mammoth physique.

"Are you saying what I do isn't real work?" The woman snarls as she abruptly flicks her cigarette in Lex's direction.

A rare smirk cracks on his steamy grimace, followed by a chuckle in his belly that does not disturb his still posture. You would assume a man with such a burly build and immense stature would be hamfisted and clumsy. Not Ser Lucious Lex. Despite his size and thickness, the man moves with grace, and his posture is always calculated. Never nervous or impulsive. Ser Lex seems to always be in a relaxed state, always focused with full awareness. If there ever is a time Lucious Lex feels fear or rage, not even an empath would sense it.

His smile melts back into a cold glare. His crow's eye squint until almost closed. "Enough games. How many of you are there?" He inquires calmly.

The woman's annoyed expression slowly turns to confused concern as she cautiously lifts her hands from the soapy water and begins to lift herself from the tub exposing her large supple breasts. "I don't know what that means, Ser Lex. But you're starting to sound cra-"

Lucious lunges with incredible reflexes like a viper from its coil and envelopes the woman's head in his massive grip. A split second of a scream is quickly muffled as Lex plunges her head to the bottom of the tub. Her legs thrash about in the air as she desperately claws aimlessly.

clung clung clung, the bronze tub reverberates with the muted banging of Lex rhythmically bludgeoning the woman's skull as she drowns. After several more minutes of struggle, the woman finally goes limp. An expulsion of a final breath leaks from her lungs and bubbles to the surface. Lex holds fast, allowing the final vestiges of life to fade with a few postmortem twitches. A greenish murk clouds the bathwater, as all of the woman's black hair detaches from her scalp and floats among the tub like tufts of seaweed. Lex hoists the woman's head from the water to inspect her face still firmly in his clutches. But staring back at him isn't the gorgeous bar room hussie he séxed moments prior. It is the lifeless face of a hairless alienoid creature. Pale white flesh stretches over an elongated ovular cranium with two bulbous black eyes and recessed nasal protrusion. Dark green blood leaks from its ebon-gummed toothless mouth.

Lex's gaze is broken by the cracking of the door being kicked in. A thin, swarthy man in a barkeep's apron comes charging into the lantern-lit and wood-paneled bathing room wielding an axe overhead. Lex leaps to his feet and hurls the shape shifter's corpse at his would-be assailant. The body awkwardly tumbles through the air and gets caught by the bite of the axe, and gets brought to the floor with the barkeep's downward chop severing its legs. The barkeep gets a firmer grip on the wooden handle to attempt to wiggle his axe from the floorboards. His effort is interrupted when he's struck across the jowls with a hard wet slap of severed leg meat. The barkeep tumbles backward into the wood-paneled wall with his arms up in a pugilistic defensive stance. Stabilized against the wall, he peers up to see a hulking, naked, and dripping wet Lex charge him, brandishing a freshly severed leg gripped around the ankle. In a frenzy of combination blows, Lex feverishly beats the barkeep. His pathetic attempts of blocking the makeshift leg-club prove useless as each strike from Lex knocks him off balance in a different direction.

Lex sways slightly to the side as a wide swing from a large meat cleaver whiffs past his face from his flank. A second assailant of eerily similar appearance cocks his arm back for another swing. Lex swiftly closes the gap before his attacker can commence a second slash. With a shoulder-lead bullrush, the still-nude Lucious violently smashes his helpless opponent against the wall to the back of him. The knife-wielding barkeep grunts with frustration as if he's being slowly crushed under the weight of a fallen auroch. He attempts to wiggle his knife hand free, but Lex immediately grips his wrist in full control. With three bruising smashes against the hardwood panel, the cleaver is knocked loose from its wielder's hand and clangs onto the stone floor with a metallic ring. The pinned barkeep winces and snarls as the hulking hero gets a full fistful of hair. With a quick wall bash against the back of the barkeep's head for good measure. Lex turns and hurls him in the opposite direction to go stumbling into the path of his compatriot now brandishing his axe freed from the floorboards. Both men collide into one another and clumsily topple to the floor.

Before either men could gain their bearings, the bare-bodied Lucious Lex looms above them, axe in hand. Lex rains down a butchering upon them before they even get a chance to react. A brief scream of horror is silenced by a vicious series of indiscriminate hacks spritzing dark green blood all over the wooden walls and stone floor. Mere seconds after death, the mangled corpses of the barkeeps begin twitching and writhing, shedding their hair and twisting into identical forms. Pale-skinned androgynous humanoids with lidless night-black spherical eyes. Jaws droop, frozen in a ghastly expression inconceivable to even the most deranged human imagination. Even the calloused Lex pauses for a moment at the unholy appearance of the changeling's inhuman form.

"They still appear manlike. The infestation must be recent. If the lord issues inquisition now he may be able to cleanse them," Ser Lex mutters to himself as he rushes over and attempts to bolt the door closed. The latching mechanism was obliterated by the first barkeep during his forced entry. Unclothed and in full flight, Lex quickly hops into his trousers, steps into his boots, and throws his dulled mail shirt over his bare torso. Like hot stones he tosses the loose pieces of platemail into his travel pack and hoists it over his shoulder. Slinking to the doorway, Lex presses his shoulder against the frame to peer out into the lantern-lit hallway. In the doorway directly adjacent to the washroom hangs a thick woolen curtain from a nailed in pig-iron rod. Lex leans his head into the doorway for a clear view into the room. He sees a moderately sized bunkroom of similar construction containing eight feather-stuffed beds with drab grey woolen blankets and worn wooden lockers at each foot. At the far end by the window, a chamberpot sits behind a makeshift privacy wall. The beds are all perfectly made and untouched. Not a soul to be found.

Lex does a swift exit maneuver from the room and begins down the hall towards the main tavern area, knees slightly bent. Each step falls softly like feline paws. Shield raised and mace tightly gripped. He leaves the short hallway to find a usually sparsely populated tavern strangely empty. The few round wooden tables and cherry-stained bar top are completely barren. Among the calm howl of the night breeze is the sound of flickering lantern flames and the slow drip of a leaky barrel tap being caught by a tin bucket. Ser Lucious creeps over to the bar to ensure no one lurks behind. All clear. All silent. He continues his way to the only feasible escape. The front door. With the front of his shield he pushes the door.open.

Thunk th-thunk thunk

A series of crossbow bolts plunge into the warrior's heater shield, completely missing his bare hand. Across the dirt road a two wheeled farmer's cart is turned on its side. From behind it a posse of unidentifiable marksmen duck down to reload their projectiles. A pair of war cries emerge from Lex's flank. Two average-sized men dressed in full chain and crudely made basket helms come charging with polearms drawn. The first pike glances off Lex's shield, then immediately recoils. Before he can block the second strike Lex let's out a thunderous groan as two crossbow bolts tear through his flesh and lodge themselves in his muscular tissue, one in his upper thigh and the other in the lower back, thus leaving a brief window for a third pike stab straight by his shield and square into his guts. The wounded hero unleashes a roar of anguish as he falls to his knee. The two fighters make a final killing lunge to finish off Ser Lex. But at the final second he raises his shield forcing each pike to glance in his off-hand direction.

With a brief second wind Lucious drives his mace in a thrusting motion up under one of the attackers helmets, driving the point through his jaw and puncturing his brain. Following through with the stab motion, Lex side steps and pirouettes behind his second enemy, catching him in the crease of his elbow for a standing rear choke. Another folly of bolts pepper the pikemen in his torso, with the final one impaling Lex's forearm and penetrating into the man's jugular. Lex hooks his mace on his belt and reaches into a small leather pouch beneath his cloak. He pulls out a handful of small acorns. Lex utters a melodic incantation and hurls the enchanted nuts through the air. As the crossbowmen pop back up for another round of shots, the acorns land in a scattered grouping all about their covered location exploding on impact. The cluster of small explosions blow them to bloody chunks and launch singed innards and mangled meat through the air to splatter onto the dirt.

Hemorrhaging blood, Lex collapses onto the ground, barely conscious. Fifty paces away sits an open stable house. He begins to crawl towards it, bleeding profusely, coughing and gasping. Over scattered gore and fresh corpses he crawls, clawing at the dirt with every last bit of strength, dragging his injured limbs as they lose feeling and function. After the wretched struggle, Ser Lucious worms under the body of his acquired horse and pitifully rolls under a divider wall into a dark corner muddied by stagnant horse shit. He lifts his head peering down at his mutilated body from the only eye he's still strong enough to hold open.

Blood spits from his mouth with a morbid chuckle. Lex slides his arms inward and places his open palms upon his wounded torso. An eerie blue glow begins to emit from his hands as he whispers melodic hymns in the old divine tongue. Slowly the blue glow subsumes his entire form, swaying and pulsating with otherworldly translucence. Lex wheezes in discomfort as his body repairs itself. Ligaments rip and reform, tendons grow and shift. His gaping wound makes the revolting sound of moist sticky meat crawling into itself as the tissues bond together and mend. Two separate clinks gently hit the stone next to him as the lodged crossbow bolts are pushed out by the healing muscular tissue rejecting the intruding matter.

Lex awakens to his boot being nudged by the opposite side of the divider wall. An abrasive beam of sunlight shines through a missing door plank forcing his eyes open. The horse nudges his boot again and loudly snorts bringing him to full consciousness. Groggy and disoriented, Lex rolls out from under the divider into a muggy, stinky horse stable. Using the trough as a crutch he brings himself to his feet. A few stiff paces brings him over to peer through the missing plank. In full daylight, the town is bustling as usual. The scene of last night's brawl in full view. No blood, no signs of damage. Even the farmer's cart has been replaced with a nearly identical one.

"They had to've heard the explosions," Lex groans with a scrunched brow.

He drops his travel pack and digs out the pieces of plate mail. Quickly he snaps, ties, and fastens every plate into place. Armor properly donned, he throws his tattered mantled cloak over his head and slings his pack over his shoulder. Lex slides the stable door wide open with his horse's reins in hand. The dozens of workers and passersby abruptly cease their tasks and conversations and in unison turn their heads towards Lex. In a brief moment of eerie silence, the entire town casts a detached, wide eyed stare at Lex. Their lips pursed into an awkward half smile. The moment passes, and all the villagers turn back to their respective doings, and the strange pause ends.

Lex briskly treks down the main dirt road of the town towards the lord's mansion. For the entire walk not a single villager, shopkeep, or guard even looks in his direction, as if he was an unseen spectre floating through an ethereal veil between worlds. Eventually, Ser Lex approaches the lord's estate–a moderate two-story tudor of red stone and beige mortar. Sprawling vines of ivy climb the entire side of the house and reach out across several trellises to canopy a small cobblestone courtyard. An old, black iron fence surrounds the perimeter with a small gate at the front guarded by a single chain-adorned soldier.

As Lex approaches the gate to ask entry, the guard, without interaction or eye contact, unlocks the iron gate and swings it open. Hesitant, Lex ties his horse and cautiously approaches the guard.

"I am Ser Lucious Lex of the Tivarian order. I must speak with your Lord."

The guard cocks his head towards Lex. His is a suntanned broad face under a kettle helm. The same expression as the villagers earlier–a mindless distant stare and alien smile.

"Yes. Please come inside," the guardsman says with an odd cheerfulness before turning his head back to looking straight ahead.

Lex carefully walks by the guard, never breaking his distrustful glare, but no other gestures are reciprocated. With his typical gaunt lumber, Lex makes his way up the cobblestone path hearing the gate latch behind him. No other movement can be seen on the property. No gardeners, housekeepers, or even playing children. Yet the estate is in pristine condition. The walkways are swept, and on either side are running flower beds with bright polychromatic petunias and begonias.

Lex climbs up the small case of stone steps to a pair of chestnut arched doors with black iron hardware. On the left side a polished bronze panel with the heraldry of a black unicorn embossed upon it. He grips the unlocked doors and pulls them open. Lex walks into a large voyeur room with painted marble floors and burning lantern sconces. From the stone walls hang various murals of noblemen and cases holding pieces of fine art. On the far side under a decorative silk canopy sits four ornate wooden chairs.

Perched in each are four immaculately dressed nobles of near identical features. Curly brown hair, fair skin and emerald green eyes. In the middle sits a father and his wife. On either side a child of similar age. One boy, one girl. The father and son are dressed in ruffled white tunics, pale green trousers, and white hose from knee to buckled black shoes. The wife and daughter are adorned in ankle-length linen skirts with sky-blue blouses. Both wear matching pearl necklaces and amber earrings. Their curly chestnut hair laying down behind their ears.

As Lex approaches, the four nobles in unison train their odd stare on his movement as he comes into earshot. In each of their unique voices, but in perfect chorus they speak, "Ser Lucious Lex. I am ever astounded at your talent to escape death. I hope your lodging accommodations were to your liking. You must be accustomed to being among piss and shit."

Lex raises his mace "I'm going to kill every last one of you changeling fiends." He growls, gritting his teeth.

In uncanny harmony, the four nobles raise their palms. "And get the reputation for murdering a noble family? I think not. Go right along causing mayhem if you'd like. It's your standard forte," they choir.

"Mayhem?! You creatures create mayhem!" Lex refutes.

Lowering their hands they maintain their blank stare and emotionless half-smile "Fiends, changelings, creatures. What colorful monikers you pathetic men conjure to justify your fear. You presuppose a plurality here, because man cannot fathom a unified state of order. By his nature, humanity in his primeval multiplicity creates only chaos."

Lex takes a few steps closer, brandishing his mace ready to strike at any moment. "What happened to the dead changelings last night? Why just let me waltz in here?" Lex asks.

"Cleaned up. It's bad for appearances to allow a monster such as you to continue quenching your thirst for carnage. Why play in your court when you have no leverage? We simply needed to pacify you" the noblemen eerily reply in ghoulish ensemble.

"I'm a monster? You fiends are a race of parasites that kill and steal the forms of men," Lex retorts.

"There you are again, incapable of wrapping your feeble intellect around the very idea of unity. Man is incapable of true peace. We are nature's desperate grasp at establishing order through singularity. We don't have ego; we don't have

rogue desires. We don't go traipsing around Grimeorth looking for wanton slaughter. That woman you murdered in the
tub. What if your intuition was wrong and you just drowned
some poor harlot? Would you feel remorse? Have you felt remorse for any of the innocent lives you've taken by mistake?
No, you chalk them up to justified casualties. But the truth of
the matter is you just kill by nature. You're a menace just like
your father," the noblemen speak coldly.

Lex whiffs his mace through the air in frustration "I'll
kill you for speaking of my father! You know nothing about
him!" Lex shouts.

"We know everything about your father and his father and his father before him. Since our descent from the
Dreamsea, we've observed man since his knuckles dragged
in the dirt. Time and time again you apes rise and fall, never
learning from your follies, repeating the same pathetic
ego-driven atrocities. There is no me or I to kill, Ser Lex. We
are woven into the very fabric of physical nature itself. From
the most diminutive to the large, any organism that carries
our blood is subsumed into the beauty of our harmonization.
And one day all living things will be replicated and replaced,
creating balance forevermore," they explain without ever
changing emotion.

Lex slowly lowers his mace as his face turns to bewil-
dered concern. "From the Dreamsea? So the lore is true.
Changelings are commanded by the mindsoul. Why not kill
and replicate me?" Lex inquires.

"Because unfortunately for you, Ser Lex, lineages such
as yours cannot be assimilated into the harmony. And killing
you would cost too much precious life. Besides, there is no
institution capable of meddling in our expansion. Consider it
silent justice allowing you to live the rest of your life know-

ing you can do nothing until you inevitably die in a scuffle with some hungry beast," they respond coldly.

"Lineages such as mine?" Lex asks with mace and shield loosely dangling at his sides.

"You had to have figured by now that your lineage had something special about it. But you're too stupid to ever uncover it. Now go. Leave us and never return. If you decide to go on a rampage, we will run and scream. Then your precious reputation as a hero will be sullied and you'll be known for the rest of your days as the bloodthirsty monster you truly are. Now go," the four nobles say in cold collective refrain as they each lift a pointed finger towards the opened mansion doors.

Lex glares at the hive-minded noblemen puppets for a few more moments before turning and storming out the doors, down the path, and out the gates. He unties his horse and begins leading it by the reins to the outskirts of town, passing by houses and workshops where villagers don't even acknowledge his presence. Lex's usual determined scowl is replaced by a lost, defeated gaze. At the town limits before the road winds off into rolling hills of grasslands, is a small storage shed stacked with bags of grain. At the corner, a small crowd of rats feeds upon a loose, open bag of grain. Lex reaches down and swiftly snatches a rat as they all scatter.

"Yes, friend. You may be right. Wherever I come from, whatever I am, I may be a monster. But I am mankind's monster."

Lex lifts the rat cupped in his massive palms to his mouth. He mutters a few terrible incantations of a blasphemous tongue and blows between his fingers onto the rat. The rodent twitches and squeaks in pain as its body bloats. Its skin twists and grows, open lesions oozing with yellow puss.

"And you speak truth, fiend. You would suffer many losses trying to slay me in battle. A battle I would surely lose. But even a monster such as I can't compete with the corpses piled by hands of lady plague."

Lex leans down and frees the sickened rat. As he mounts his horse and gallops off, the diseased vermin scurries through the nooks and narrows of the homes and workshops and into the heart of the village.

The Chronicles of Count Choralure
Volume 1: The Crypt of Carnonwe
by A. Cuthbertson

In the dimly-lit doorway of the crypt, a crooked figure leaned on a gnarled staff. At his feet was a lantern, sputtering as the last embers of its flame died down. The figure paid it no heed – he had brought it more out of habit than anything. The more he advanced in his craft, the less he needed the light. He'd taken to avoiding daylight altogether, if possible. The night was his realm now.

From the dank darkness below, there came unsettling scrabbling and scraping sounds. The figure looked over his shoulder, as though making sure that nobody else was around to hear it. There was indeed nobody - the figure stood in an abandoned graveyard, far east of the city of Sorrowhorle, deep in the saltwater Sorrowhorle Swamps. Much further east lay an inland sea named the Adrince Ocean.

The graveyard was so overgrown with vines and moss that the tombstones underneath could barely be seen. It was in a small, flat patch surrounded on all sides by steep hills, with trees growing so tall around them that the area was draped in a permanent green gloom. There was an iron gate across a small dip in the hills, which had been rusted shut for decades. An inscription above the gate could no longer be read, and the wrought ironwork songbirds either side looked sad and starved of sunlight.

There was one thing that could be seen clearly despite the overgrowth: the crypt at the far end of the cemetery. This was the Crypt of Carnonwe, a Knight of the Alabaster Order, which had been all but forgotten by the peasants in the local towns. Even the folk who inhabited the larger city of Sorrowhorle had mostly forgotten the crypt's location. It was on maps, but most people had no need for maps - they stayed put.

This particular graveyard had long been abandoned, and not only because the Order had fallen out of favour with the peasantry. There were many reasons to avoid graveyards after the events that the Alabaster Order had started in motion at Werevar Castle a century ago. At first, there were only outlandish reports of fiends in the night, of folk turning up pale and drained of blood, and of odd strangers hanging around outside of town at night... and they loved graveyards and anywhere else that the dead congregated.

As the years went by, farmers, and anyone living in isolated communities without adequate protection, started to disappear in the night. Trader caravans travelling overnight would not arrive at their destinations. Towns and cities were cut off from one another. Nevertheless, over an entire century, news travelled between them, and the entire Westerlands began to be regarded as cursed territory.

Now, a whole continent lived in terror. People burned their dead. Some folk even burned those that were only *sus-*

pected to be dead. They might scream, but that could be just another devilish trick played by those ever-present nocturnal hunters: the Drained. Better to be safe than sorry.

This made the crooked figure's craft much more difficult. For him, it was much better to have real, tangible remains... flesh, bone, sinew. Normally, he'd be digging up as much as he could from a goldmine like this, even if the remains were old. "Fresh is best," as he'd taken to muttering to himself, but even bones and ancient desiccated flesh would do. Regardless, he paid the other graves no heed. The real treasure tonight was to be found in the Crypt of Carnonwe.

Carnonwe, although a member of that ill-fated old Order, was a famous Knight indeed. The legends spoke of his glimmering silver sword, shield, and suit of armour. He'd no doubt been buried with much else besides. Some gold and maybe even some jewels, perhaps decorative ornaments and tools. These were of no interest, besides maybe being able to fence them at a later date - what the crooked man was after was that silver.

Silver was a certain way to kill certain creatures stone dead, and if one had the know-how, it could be used in dark rituals to wreak great havoc and misery upon them. For that very reason, it was hard to come by. The Drained could sense the presence of silver from miles around - and these days, they were never too far away. Despite their aversion to it, they would come in great numbers, to make sure that no humans could come and use it against them.

The Crypt itself was deeply cursed with their foul magicks. No mortal, living man could step inside - his lungs would fill with blood, he would die a horrible death, and his corpse would provide a raucous feast for the Drained that were alerted to his trespassing.

That's why the crooked figure stood in the doorway - he was no Drained. He was, as yet, a living man. He could not cross the threshold. Advanced in his craft as he was, he could sense death awaiting him inside, a barrier no more than six inches in front of him. This was why he'd sent his servants in. They didn't need to worry about the death magick of the Drained.

His servants were dead already.

The crooked figure was none other than the estranged Count Choralure, widely rumoured to have delved into the dark arts of Necromancy many years ago. He had been driven out of his family's estate, as a result of the populace's warranted fear of the undead.

Choralure couldn't blame them, but those vigilant villagers had made his work much harder. In Castle Choralure, he had a laboratory, a protected trade route to the village to bring supplies, a chapel with a graveyard... and a very trusting populace.

Trust can only last so long, though. Especially in the Westerlands. He had overstretched. He dwelled on this part of his past frequently, but the ancient tomes that he had procured all gave the same guidance: for one to pursue the path of Necromancy, one must never get too comfortable.

In fact, one must overcome their deepest revulsions to pursue it. In order to prepare the dark rituals required to raise the dead, one must dig through rotten entrails to acquire the foulest remnants of decay. One must extract the most putrid corpse-ichors and use them to brew the foulest potions, and one must learn to imbibe them without gagging or dying of the subsequent illnesses. The closer they brought one to death, the better... but one could not continue if one actually died.

Not so early in the process, anyway.

46

Count Choralure had completed these preliminary processes in his castle, but when the time came, he had to leave. He'd known it was coming - there were too many rumours flying around the village unchecked. He'd been careless, and his appearance had grown more ghoulish as he drank his potions and performed his vile rites. Eventually, disappearances that weren't even his fault began to be blamed on him.

One day, at the crack of dawn, the villagers came up the hill toward Castle Choralure armed with a battering ram, oil, torches, and all the weapons they could find.

Before leaving through secret tunnels dug into the mountain-side, he'd loaded up his most trustworthy servant, Prospero, with his most prized possessions: the three tomes of Necromantic lore that he had emptied the family coffers to acquire. Many men had died to acquire these tomes for him... and he hoped that many more would die as a result of their acquisition.

Despite this, the Count did not view himself as an evil man. He was living a life of evil, he knew, but his motives were good. He sought to rid the world of the Drained, the only way he knew how... by playing them at their own game. If it took an army of the dead to beat an army of the dead, then so be it.

The living had had a whole century, and they had done nothing except capitulate and lose ground. In order for them to survive at all, something had to be done. Somebody had to step in, and Count Choralure saw himself as that unlikely hero: a man who would be burned at the stake if he was caught by the living, but who nevertheless fought for their very survival.

The difference between him and the Drained, he told himself, was that he would stop when he was done.

Count Choralure's mind had wandered quite enough. He had fond memories of his time at Castle Choralure, before he and Prospero had to run, but he knew those memories were a sign of weakness. He had to cut ties and fully embrace the darkness of his new life - even if he missed certain parts of that life quite dearly.

His servant Prospero, for example. Never had he met a more useful, obedient, and loyal man than Prospero. He still met all of those criteria... but back then, Prospero had more life in him. He was a conversationalist, a man to bounce ideas off. And he was much funnier when he was alive.

After the scraping noises had finished in the Crypt below, Prospero came slopping up the stairs. Choralure looked sadly at the remnants of his face.

The flesh covering it was yellow-greenish, decaying, and almost sloughing off his cheeks in rivulets. There were flies and maggots crawling all over him. His jaw hung slack. One eye was glazed milky white, and the other still as brilliantly blue as it had ever been.

Prospero deserved better, Choralure thought, and this was one recurring regret that he could not quite shake off. If only he had more *time*, more practice, then he could have really made an effort with Prospero. The servant's incredible loyalty to him and his cause could have been put to such better use... but here he was, a waddling wreck that the Count did not yet have a heart blackened enough to abandon.

Still, though, Prospero had proven very useful. More useful than Choralure's second servant, anyway, who came padding up the stairs afterwards and stood at the top of them next to Prospero.

This one had no name - naming them was strictly forbidden by the tomes. Prospero had kept his name as a result of the attachment they'd shared beforehand - but Choralure knew that the day should come when Prospero would become just another mass of shuffling flesh, an anonymous face in the horde.

His second servant was newer. Fresher. Count Choralure had improved, had advanced in the craft, before raising this one. The man was a woodcutter that Choralure had found injured in the forest. He had taken the man back to his lair, under the pretence of fixing him up, but had slowly fed the man potions which led him further and further to the gates of death. All the while, Choralure had been drawing the necessary circles and symbols under his bed, preparing the foul incense, chanting the rites...

When the time came, he had a perfectly healthy, fresh corpse. All the preparations were complete - he was raised almost immediately after passing. This one was almost too fresh, though... he was unruly. Choralure feared that the control over this one would break. He hadn't quite the necessary power or skill to raise one so strong and so healthy - but one could never be sure how advanced one was in the craft without trying one's luck.

The raised woodcutter looked at Choralure with hooded eyes, as though with scorn. He was a handsome man, showing almost no signs of being dead apart from his pale skin and muteness. The woodcutter's jaw, unlike Prospero's, was firm and gritted. His hands were held out.

The Count looked down to see what he held. Nothing but gold-threaded necklaces and copper rings encrusted with jewels. Choralure tutted. He looked to Prospero then, who held out a sack. He peered inside and smiled.

"Yes," he said quietly, "you beautiful man, you've found exactly what I wanted…" there was the unmistakable green-tinted glint of old silver. It didn't look like there was quite as much as the legends said - there never is, he thought. But there was more than enough for his current requirements.

The helmet and the sword and the armour clanked around in the sack as Choralure gave Prospero the mental command to wrap it up. He commanded the woodcutter to drop his handfuls of treasure into the sack too.

"What are we going to do with you," the Count muttered, "strong as a horse but dumb as a rock…"

At this, the woodcutter's eyebrows flickered. Was that a frown, Choralure asked himself? He was perturbed. That shouldn't happen. He would have to get rid of this one, he thought. This one was too risky to keep around.

He had considered giving the order to retrieve Carnon-we's corpse, but he knew better than to try to raise a member of the Alabaster Order so early on his path. It was that kind of thing that had got the Westerlands into this mess in the first place: the dread severing of man's spirit which the Order performed at Werevar Castle. Choralure didn't know what would happen if a ritual on such an unhallowed corpse went awry, but nevertheless, he had made a note of this location on his map and was determined to return much, much later.

Anyway, it was time to go. The Drained would be alerted to the missing silver quite soon, although the Count and his compatriots would have a head-start: the Drained knew there was a concentrated amount of silver in the area already. It would be a while before they realised that it was moving.

The Count gave the order, and they shuffled towards the gate of the graveyard. The stronger of his thralls pulled aside the rusted gates for his master and Prospero to pass and closed it behind them. The three of them proceeded slowly down into the swamp. Prospero wasn't very quick off the mark anyway, but the Count even less so.

In an odious ritual performed at the last full Moon, Choralure had given forth some of his life's essence to advance along the path. He had spent the whole month beforehand preparing reagents and rehearsing the steps of the ritual, and he'd been successful, but he had paid a heavy price.

When working towards these goals, he'd ask Prospero for his thoughts. The putrefying manservant would stare at him blankly, as always, in silence.

"Hmm, yes, quite," would come Choralure's response, "but how do you think the author intended that phrase to be pronounced? Really, you think so?"

In this way, the maddened Count would conduct entire conversations with his silent partner. Choralure would often sigh deeply. He missed his old friend. During Prospero's life, he'd share ideas and plans with the man, and relish his witty responses. After his death and subsequent raising, he hadn't said a word. Now, the Count would laugh aloud at imagined quips, or deliver black-humoured jokes himself, alone in his lair, with nobody but the silent, stinking dead for an audience.

After this last ritual had concluded, Choralure found that his legs withered at an alarming rate. He now walked with a staff, not for magickal purposes, but to support his weight. The staff had been carved with sinister sigils, but had not yet been charged, so it was simply dead wood. The charging and enchanting would come when the moon reached its height again, and some of Choralure's newly-procured silver would help make it a very powerful Necromantic conduit indeed.

Every step pained Choralure now, but pain was merely another barrier to overcome on the Path. He had a mad idea for some kind of palanquin to be carried upon on quests like these, but he'd need a couple of strong thralls... strong *obedient* thralls, he thought to himself, eyeing the woodcutter with suspicion. The woodcutter stared at him unnervingly as he hobbled through the swamp. Not straight ahead... but straight *at him*.

An ear-splitting shriek made Count Choralure wince. "Bastards," he said aloud, and looked around left-to-right in panic. The Drained! He couldn't run in his weakened state; he was far away from achieving his palanquin idea, never mind the augmentations that could be gained toward the end of the Path. He cursed himself for attempting a mission as dangerous as this in person, whilst being so weak. Raiding this tomb would have been better performed much later down the Path, when he would be able to mentally control multiple undead thralls from a much greater distance.

But silver was a necessary reagent to advance to that stage, and it was so hard to come by... he had used all of the family silver in the Castle, and much of the surrounding villagers' too, to perform his preliminary dedications and rituals. That meant he had probably left those villagers wide open to an attack by the Drained, he realised, but sacrifices had to be made. He was thinking about the bigger picture.

The shrieking grew louder, but Choralure realised that it was not the gleeful shriek of the hunter zoning in on its prey. This one was a shriek of pain... he could hear reeds being trampled and swamp-water splashing. The Count and his two thralls walked off the path and into the reeds. He crouched down, hidden, and watched keenly.

There, thirty feet away, came a black shadow bolting out of the green. The figure was running at high speed, but it appeared to have a limp. It tripped over in the swampy water, and splashed around. Choralure saw its face - pale, whitish-grey skin pulled tightly over its skull like leather on a drum. A mouth full of deadly-sharp teeth. And eyes like long, horizontal slits, with bright red pupils. And a look that he'd never before seen on one of their faces - true fear.

In hot pursuit came a gang of men - living men - with ropes and nets. Choralure realised that the creature in the water had a rope tied around one leg… but why on Earth was it running? Four normal men were no match for even one of the Drained, thought the Count.

The man in front drew his sword, and Choralure gasped. Glittering in the gloom was a sword of the purest silver, with an ornately carved hilt, and a savagely long and sharp blade. The man pointed the sword at the creature's chest and looked down at it pitilessly, his long golden hair cascading onto his broad chest in great flowing locks.

"No!" rasped the Drained, trying to scramble away, "no! I can help you!"

The man sneered. He said, in a commanding voice, "the desperate pleas of the already-dead. You have clung on to life for far too long, creature. Who knows how many men you have killed and drank dry in your time?"

"None!" screamed the creature, writhing under his gaze.

One of the other men walked around to secure the rope around the creature. Suddenly, the thing lashed out with its claws, pulling the man by the waist toward itself and then throwing him at the ringleader's sword. The man cried out in pain as he was impaled, and the Drained sank its teeth into the man's shoulder, taking care to avoid the silver weapon poking through his chest.

There were a few awkward movements as the blonde-haired man struggled to withdraw his sword from his comrade, giving the thing a precious few seconds to drink. Choralure watched with fascination as all colour drained immediately from its victim, and he fell into the swamp, limp and pale and dead.

After drinking the man's blood, a change came over the Drained: its eyes glowed redder, it stood taller, its stance was mean and wily, it moved quicker. It ducked down and rolled away while chewing through the rope with its razor-sharp teeth, severing it almost immediately. It leapt, an amazing feat considering the distance, onto one of the other hapless men who screamed and went down under its toothy assault.

"Sivrite!" cried the last man, "do something!"

"That's *Sir* Sivrite to you, knave!" the blonde man said imperiously. He rushed to the aid of the man who had shouted.

Very good, thought Choralure, he runs to the man who's *next* to be attacked, rather than try to save the one who's clearly dead already… this Sivrite must have experience. He knew that the fiend would be unable to control its appetite in such an orgy of bloodshed, and would soon be upon the next man who did not carry silver.

Sivrite reached the last man in time - just as the Drained was reaching out with one pale crooked claw, he brought his sword up in a sweeping motion and severed the thing's outstretched hand. The hand flew in an arc toward, by chance, Count Choralure and his two silent companions. Choralure looked at the hand, floating there tantalisingly in front of him, bobbing around in the bog, claw bent as though beckoning him forward to take it.

An intact hand of one of the Drained… a very valuable and scarce resource. Normally these things didn't even die, never mind give up their body parts to Necromancers. It was a plucky man indeed who set out to hunt the Drained, rather than cower in his shack, hoping that the family heirloom half-silver ring he clutched would be enough to protect him.

Choralure looked back up to see Sivrite plunging his sword into the fiend's chest, drawing out the most terrible screech. That's sure to bring a *lot* more of them, thought Choralure, as he watched the thing wriggle and writhe and begin to burn from the chest outward.

Sivrite obviously thought so too, as he and his friend left the burning creature and paced warily around, looking in all directions. Sivrite clutched the sword tightly. He stood up to his full height, puffed out his chest, and shouted, "Come on then, you freaks!"

After issuing this challenge, he laughed maniacally.

"That man's insane," Choralure said quietly, "don't you think so, Prospero?"

Prospero looked at him silently. A worm slid over the socket of his milky eye.

"Yes," Choralure muttered, "quite…"

From deper in the swamp, there came a crashing and a smashing. The Count cowered in the reeds with his two silent thralls, while Sivrite grinned and adopted a rangy fighting stance. Curiously, the Count thought, these noises were not accompanied by the trademark shrieking and howling of the Drained… the noises grew louder. Whatever it was sounded *big*.

Something large came sailing over the treetops. In the pale swamp-light, it was hard to make out, but it was heading straight for the area where Sivrite and his man were standing. They leaped out of the way just in time, and the item came down with an almighty splash in the water around their feet.

Choralure peered from his spot in the reeds. It appeared to be an entire medium-sized tree, roots and branches splayed out like twisted limbs, which had been wholly uprooted.

Sivrite and his man looked at each other for a moment, mouths agape. Then, with a deep, gurgling roar, a gargantuan shape charged out of the treeline. Sivrite cursed, and his man dropped his ropes and nets in fear. A stench came over the area that made the eyes water; even Count Choralure, who wore the reek of putrefaction as his permanent perfume, wrinkled his nose in disgust.

"Swamp troll, Sir Sivrite!" the smaller man shouted.

"I see that, knave!" came the reply.

The troll drew itself up to its full height. It was three times the height of the brave Sir Sivrite, and many times more wide. The creature's corpulent bellies rolled outward and down, reaching the water, and its hideous face was covered in warts. The thing's mouth was massive, easily able to chew the knight in two bites, although most of its teeth had rotted away, and the few that were left poked upward like grime-encrusted tombstones from blackened muddy gums.

Its eyes fixed on Sivrite's glittering sword, two massive, wild eyeballs with slit-pupils, and it gave out another roar. It reached forward with its finned arms and tried to grab the knight. Sivrite ducked and rolled out of the way, trying to lash out with the sword as he rose, but he missed the troll's hand by mere inches. The troll growled in frustration and punched outward with its other hand, which connected with Sivrite's companion's face. The man's neck was snapped in an instant.

Sivrite howled in rage, having seen all of his companions die in this accursed swamp, and charged at the troll headlong. He stabbed out at the thing's hideous head, but it drew back its neck instinctively, exposing its fat belly. The sword sank

56

into the soft flesh. Sivrite set one foot behind him and took a hard lunge forward with the other foot, so that the sword bit deep and slashed through the troll's belly in a wide arc.

The contents of the troll's foul belly, blood and pus and many liquids even more disgusting than those, sprayed out into Sivrite's face. The man screamed in disgust and the troll howled in pain. The beast wasn't done yet, and it shuffled backward and readied itself for another assault.

The Count, although thoroughly entertained, saw his opportunity to leave. He and his two thralls walked out of the reeds and began to head out of the swamp. He knew he'd be safe - Sivrite and the swamp troll were making so much noise that any vile creatures for miles around would be attracted to their position, rather than his own.

Choralure remembered the severed hand of the Drained, and turned back to grab it and stuff it into his pocket. He made a splash in the swamp-water as he did so. This caught Sivrite's attention.

The man darted his head toward the Count, and he frowned in confusion. He saw the two undead thralls beside him and was instantly on guard, changing his position so that he could see both Choralure and the swamp troll at the same time.

While the Count was under no illusion that Sivrite would kill him if he had the chance, he saw great potential in the brave young knight. And he had an unruly minion to be rid of, after all: the woodcutter. With great mental effort, he directed the raised corpse towards the troll.

The woodcutter made a gurgling noise in protest, as its limbs snapped and jerked, and it walked unwillingly into the path of the troll. With an evil look backward at the Count, as though to let him know that the Necromancer controlled only his body and not his mind, the woodcutter broke into a run and dived at the swamp monster.

The troll held its belly-wound with one hand and tried to swat the woodcutter away. The woodcutter scratched and bit at it, until the troll was forced to grip him with both hands, and lift him bodily upward. The troll tried to rip the woodcutter's head from his shoulders, while the woodcutter bit and snarled.

Sivrite, although very confused, saw his opportunity to strike. He ran at the troll, bellowing a harrowing battle-cry.

With this, Count Choralure turned away, and continued out of the swamp. In his pocket, he held a rare ritual reagent, and in one of Prospero's hands was the sack of silver and jewels. He felt the mental link to the woodcutter weakening as energy left the thrall's body, which returned some strength to his legs. He was able to pick up his pace slightly.

Plus, he thought happily, the brave knight would not have to deal with a feral undead after he'd dealt with the troll - the troll would soon kill the woodcutter. Everything had been tied up rather neatly, and the Count was making off with more treasure than he'd expected to.

He felt that this was not the last he'd see of the courageous, golden-haired Sir Sivrite with the silver sword. Their paths were very different, but their goals were clearly the same - to rid these Westerlands of the Drained scourge that had befallen them. He was more than a match for an injured swamp troll, the Count hoped, but he was not going to wait around to find out.

In Prospero's other hand was the ankle of Sivrite's companion, the dead squire with the snapped neck. Choralure needed another thrall to replace the woodcutter, after all, and this man had been fit, healthy, and brave. Prospero dragged the corpse through the swamp-water, following his hobbling master, w the shouts and gruesome gurgles of combat rang out behind them.

60

There Ain't No Pleasing You
Aaron Robert Giesen

The spirit entered my mouth with a warm welcome despite the foul burning sensation that I hadn't yet gotten used to. A lot less palatable than the weak Fruit Seltzers they allowed back on Earth, but it hit the spot more far more efficiently, and I could drink as much as I wanted! The simulated evening-sun-emulating bulbs faded to a sunset red as I took my seat in the command chair. *Some position of command,* I thought. As usual I knew the debrief was going to bore me to tears, it was so rare that anything actually required my attention. It was the only time I ever allowed the bots to use their voices. It was easy for me to ignore their insipid reporting over a glass of whatever I'd managed to distill in the med-bay this week. I couldn't bring myself to read status reports while drunk; I was already half blind before I even brewed my first batch. I'm surprised I managed to hide my poor eyesight during the medical for this assignment.

I paid what little attention I could muster just to get by. Three more days and this would all be over. By Science, I hated those droning voices! Not human enough to engage me, but also too human for the kind of solace that I craved.

"Engine room running at 72.9% capacity…" *So running then?*

"…Decks 4 through 7 are unsanitary, please replace disinfectant lines…" - *I don't use those decks, next?*

"…We are running low on synthetic yeast in the kitchen, please check for leaks in the supply line to the baker-bot…" - *Yep, there's a leak all right, straight to my med-bay distillery.*

"…We regret that we are still unable to fully repair the navigation systems to reach Ellipsi-12 for the mining mission. By default we will return to Corporate deep space HQ station in approximately 3 solar cycles for system debugging…" - *Oh I certainly hope so…*

The report chugged along, painfully. Each sentence more bearable than the last, no doubt this was helped along by what I believe used to be called "vodka" in the pre-ACC days of our intolerable civilisation.

"…finally an anomaly has been detected 0.23 parsecs from our destination…" This grabbed my attention momentarily. "…this should not require any alterations to our course; however, we are not able to fully confirm without full functionality of our nav-systems." *Never mind then, we're still good to go.*

I'd spent every corporate credit I had faking the medical to get this assignment. Not that I harboured any aspirations of command, if you could call this command, I just needed away from Earth. Controlled fun, controlled socialising, controlled walks in the controlled forest. The tree here in the Oxy-deck was *mine* and I could spend as long as I bloody well wanted around it. The last few centuries had whittled what was once called Mother Earth's final remnants of humanity down to nothing.

My home had become a feudalist corporate battleground, its denizens comfortable, sedentary and bland. Not a real battleground either – violence had essentially been wiped out for nearly a century. More of a battleground of mergers and acquisitions, and the most we lowly consumers would notice would be a different logo on our corporate credits. I'd read about how the machines had begun to take all of the work sometime around the 21st century, back when we used to gauge time based on a deity's supposed birthday. It started quite innocuously: food market employees reduced to watching over machines, occasionally changing a till roll here and fixing an error there.

I found it funny that since all those years ago humanity's role was basically the same. Stagnated, reduced, subsistent. The thought made me sick. This "command role" was just that too, watching the bots work and occasionally changing a disinfectant line or something equally menial, not that I would if I could avoid it. I wasn't here to work. This had become my permanent vacation.

It had crept up on me, the permanence of whatever this plan was. At first I just wanted to get away for as long as possible, and a long-haul deep-space mining assignment seemed to be perfect for this. Crew numbers on these vessels had been reduced to one years ago, with ships programmed to return to the nearest HQ in the event of death or injury. This neutered role paid well enough to account for its solitary aspect, but I'd have done this for free.

Here I was, alone with my tree in my metal carapace, with incredible cupola views that no scientific explanation could quantify. Free from inane chatter about the most recent corporate-approved dating show or VR vacation experience. Strangely, I was closer to nature here alone with my tree in deep space than I was anywhere on my home planet. Over time the desire for solitude gradually turned to apathy, which turned to alcoholism, which turned to anger and bitterness.

I grew weary of having to interact with the bots even in the most menial ways. Of having to order my meals cooked *for* me and not by me and always so annoyingly perfect! Of having to sit through those damn reports! My solitude was no longer lonely enough. Then one day in a drunken stupor, stumbling through the corridors of my escape-vessel-turned-prison, I was struck with the desire to punch those corporate overlords in the face. But faceless corporations don't have faces. So in lieu of a face I decided to punch them right in the bridge of their corporate HQ with all 80,000 metric tonnes of this expensive mining vessel. A blaze of glory to inject some excitement into my life and some sort of justice into the universe. A poignant end that would satisfy my most self indulgent romanticisations, sweetened along the way by every prohibited sip of my self-made liquor. *Self-made.*

The realisation that I had essentially become a terrorist had occurred to me long after my decision to set this in motion. I had laughed long and hard for what seemed like days when it struck me. But this was no crusade for any real cause, I just couldn't stomach going back to Earth. And to fuck over those profit-driven sociopaths that considered themselves oh-so un-fuckable, however temporarily, would also be a nice bonus. So few people would actually be aboard corporate HQ, and in my mind they were dead already in every way that counts. My mind was set. Emergency docking procedures allowed a 15-second human override, more than enough time to cause some serious damage.

The next two and a half days blew by with a serene calm-

ness. The bots no longer bothered me; I found myself joking-
ly conversing with them about topics I knew they wouldn't
understand, love and beauty and the like. I even tried once
or twice to get them to acknowledge that dogmatic faith in
science was just as crude as the religions that its followers
had wiped out. They wouldn't accept the hypocrisy, I got the
same response every time, said with an irritating politeness:

"Science is truth, please reconsider your judgment. This
heresy has been noted in your file and you will be scheduled
for re-socialisation upon return to Earth." I laughed each
time; I knew I wasn't going back to Earth, and it felt so good
to speak freely for once. I imagined bemusement on their
behalf in a humanising way. It struck me how we humans felt
a compulsion to anthropomorphise objects like this just to be
able to interact with machines. 452 years A(fter)C(orporate)
C(larity), and they still hadn't driven out all of our humanising impulses! At least, not mine.

I spent hours skipping around my tree like it was a maypole, like in some archaic ceremony I'd read about once. It
was more fun than all the birthdays and corporate sanctioned
social events I'd ever been to. I could barely contain my glee
as the time ticked by. I sang and laughed and joked like a
madman. Perhaps I *had* lost my mind; it didn't matter. The
anticipation bubbled up within me, and I felt like an excited
child. It was strange how such innocent feelings could spring
from such a sinister plan.

There were hundreds of messages on the comm system
from HQ. I had disabled my ability to respond long before
coming into range. It was simple enough to do, a water
spillage into the bridge microphones and then beating the
repair bot into scrap before it could do its only duty and fix
them. Before I did it, I had hoped to revel in some primal
rush straight from my amygdala, but it felt more like fixing

a machine despite being the exact opposite. It perturbed me to think that my rogue 15-second crash course might be just as numb of an experience. I shook off this feeling with a long swig of vodka and an involuntary shudder. I convinced myself that the added element of taking 3 or 4 living breathing creatures down with me might add something a little more substantial to the carnage. I felt shocked at this line of thought, albeit briefly. I realised that I'd taken this whole venture a lot further than originally intended. It was too late now though and there was no going back. *I couldn't go back.*

I'd programmed a text response to auto-respond to HQ's hails:

<NAV SYSTEM AND COMM SYSTEM MALFUNCTION. ALIVE AND WELL. DOCKING FOR REPAIRS - MANUAL DOCKING REQUIRED. LOOKING FORWARD TO RE-SOCIALISATION.>

I watched one or two of their holo-messages with their dull, irritating tone and patronising, rehearsed body language and washed it down with more of my vodka. I got the feeling they were suspicious of how the ship had gotten into such a state, but they weren't about to let a ship this expensive go. They needed a return on their investment, or at the very least to mitigate some of their losses. *And some loss it was going to be.* They had expressed their own brand of concern about my wellness status report. The kind of concern that says they care about my wellness and how helpful my impending re-socialisation would be, but that *meant*, "get back in line, insect."

Well I'm no insect, I am the biggest pest in all the hive.

Suddenly, the ship's red alert sounded. I raced to the bridge, cursing myself thinking I had let the ship fall into too much disrepair to reach my target so close to arriving. I threw myself into the command chair and shouted for a status report from the nav-bot.

"Anomaly appears to be a unique singularity. Mid-range scanners were unable to determine the severity of the object's negative mass and natural tractor field due to its size. The ship is on a collision course and will encounter the anomaly in T-minus 26 minutes 12 seconds. We are unable to determine the exact consequences."

I began to panic. *A unique singularity? What did that even mean?* I frantically paced and begged the bots to do *something*, try *anything*. Every time I received the same response.

"Collision unavoidable and imminent, please repair communications and issue SOS to HQ." I knew I couldn't, I'd killed the comms repair bot. *Killed, there I go humanising again.*

Each time I begged for help the same response was parroted back to me, until I noticed that, ever so slightly, it seemed like the bot's speech was slower every time they spoke. I felt like I was imagining it and that maybe it was the stress and adrenaline warping my perception. I asked again. Surely It couldn't be slower? The corporation had settled on the pace and intonation of bot voices to maximise compliance in humans years ago, this was standardised across all machines. I asked again and again.

"Cccooollllllliiisssiiiooonnn uuunnnaaavvvoooii-idddaaabbbllleee aaannnddd iiimmmiiinn-neeeennnttt pppllleeeaaassseee rrreeepppaaaiiirrr cccooooommmmmmmmmuuuunnnniiiicccccaaaattttiiiio-ooonnnnssss aaaaannnnnddddd iiiiisssssssssssuuuuueeeee SSSSSSOOOOOOOSSSSSS TTTTTTOOOOOO HHHHHH-QQQQQQ"

Doubting my tenuous sanity, it took me far longer than

it should have to decide to check the collision timer. There it was! Each second longer than the last, already taking what seemed to me like 5 seconds, then 10, then 20. By the time I had calmed myself enough to count the seconds as closely as I could, each second lasted, by my count, 1 minute according to the timer, and they were slowing exponentially. The nav-bot's speech had slowed to a distorted drone, spending what felt like forever on each word, their movements slow and sluggish.

I grabbed a hand console and left the bots to their increasingly reduced motion and their unbearable droning. This had become too much for me, and the best that I could come up with was that I needed a drink, and I needed my tree. I staggered through the corridors, swallowing as much vodka as I could without being sick and headed for the Oxy-deck, to my tree. I sat down, exhausted and defeated. According to the hand console, the time of collision was T-minus 19 minutes 6 seconds. I couldn't keep a mental count of each second anymore so I gave up. I slumped down on my maypole tree, accepted whatever fate had in store, and passed out.

I woke up feeling well rested, hungover but well rested. Certainly hours later, according to how my biological clock *felt*. It seemed that this was the only reliable sense of time that I now had. I had bought my good grades along with the fake medical clearance - *another expensive lie to get me here* - but I had a limited understanding of singularity theories and experimental physics from my time in the corporate academy, not that I paid much attention.

I guessed that the anomaly must have been distorting time. *Or maybe just my perception of it?* I had no real idea. Somehow all the ship's tech and bots' processing rate had slowed in line with the time distortion. By now the clock had been stuck on 19 minutes and 1 second for longer than I could bear to look. Each time I checked it was the same, and I could feel it pushing my sanity to the edge. *How was I unaffected?*

Every time I looked at the timer I was overcome with pure frustration. I drank more and more and flew into a blind rage. I tore down the thickest branch from my tree and I toured the ship tearing out the vocal box of every droning bot I came across, silencing their maddening cacophony. I smashed every console screen in sight with my branch. It was poetic, two forces of nature working in tandem to overcome technology. I felt more alive than I ever had in my entire life. The last screen was my hand console, and its timer ticked down one second to 19 minutes exactly, just before my branch shattered the screen. I thought for a moment that I should care about this, but I couldn't bring myself to. I was in a state of adrenaline-induced bliss. I returned to my tree, collapsed, and fell into the soundest sleep I had ever experienced.

An amount of time has passed. Time no longer means anything to me so I can't say how long it has been, if it has moved at all. My perception of it gauged by my body clock is no longer serving any purpose. I have read once about the Buddah, an old deity that reached a state of ego death and timelessness under a tree, was this me? Had that been a prophecy? I didn't move from my spot under my tree. Why would I? Both the tree and I seem to have stopped ageing. All observable bodily functions have gone. I no longer feel hunger or the need to eat, but I process thoughts at the same rate as I always did, maybe even faster, I can't tell. I have no metric of time.

I no longer need to move from this spot, I don't know when I will again. I sit beneath my tree, and when I sleep I lie beneath my tree. I sleep, but I sleep from mental exhaustion alone, to dream. My dreams stretch on for millennia. All the data, movies, books, everyone I have ever seen or met, everything is available to me at my command. I dream in per-

fect lucidity, and I have mastered control of this to the point where I feel truly transcendent.

I am beyond the Buddah. When I wake, I can call upon the knowledge and experience gained from my dreams to the point where it is almost impossible to tell the difference between being awake and asleep. I haven't moved in an amount of time that can be comprehended by human or machine, yet my muscles have not atrophied, and I still feel no hunger. I do not tire or want for anything.

I am my first stolen kiss in re-education camp. I am the crimson glow of the morning sun under a rare natural sky. I am the unstoppable motion of the wind between the city spires. I am the forest reservation I visited as a child, and I am each ring I counted on the tree stump within. I am all the love I have ever given or received, that was free from corporate control; I am the subtle moments of shared humanity I found with others in its grasp. I am unfettered by the nuances of control that once dampened my experience as a sensory being. I am the hero in all of my favourite tales. I am silence, and I am beauty. I breathe in the good; I exhale the bad. This is all I ever wanted and more. Solitude to call upon at any time, or anything I could imagine in any way I want it to be. All my bitterness melted away aeons ago. I began to forget how or why I reached this Godhood. Whether or not I deserved this was immaterial. I was immaterial. I was the tree, and the tree was me. As above, so below...

...A leaf landed on my face and woke me. I felt fuzzy and somewhat hungover. *Was this a dream? Why would I dream up a hangover?* I walked with an unfamiliar lethargy to the command room, bemused that I had to stop to throw up and drink water. *This must be a dream, but why am I not in control of it?*

I reached the command centre. I remembered something about a version of myself from a long time ago - *wait, time means something to me?* - destroying the nav-bot's voice box and smashing screen consoles.

I rerouted the nav-bots functions through the holo-comm system. An image of the ship's collision course came up on the holo-field, and the nav-bot was repeating the same line over and over.

"Collision course was successfully navigated. Ship has been safely but inexplicably displaced 14.87 parsecs from the anomaly's location. Engines overloaded. Please repair communications and issue SOS to the nearest Corporate rescue ship"

I struggled to piece together what had happened. Questions raced through my mind faster than I could address them. What had it meant *displaced*? Had time been passing all the while? How had we moved? Was the singularity some sort of wormhole? I was halfway through trying to coherently type my questions to the nav-bot when the holo-comms flashed up with an incoming hail. I was confronted by the corporate logo glowing in a harsh blue light above the holo-comm projector and was struck with dread. I answered the hail but could not speak.

A pompous figure illuminated the room and spoke in a practiced tone of voice that brought back every inch of bitterness that I had given up so long ago:

"We received your auto message, so we understand we won't be able to hear you. But rest assured, we are on our way to pick you up. It seems your manual docking controls are down along with your engines, so we'll have to board you and make some repairs. We have no idea how you got here, your ship is scheduled to be most of its way to Ellipsi-12!

Don't worry, you're only two days out from Earth, so once you're aboard we'll get you a hot meal, a sedative, and ship you straight to the re-socialisation centre. Glad to hear that you're looking forward to it!"

I sat in blissful disbelief for a moment until the reality of the situation came crashing down. Then, throwing up, I was overcome with shock, then horror, then grief for what I had lost, before finally settling into perfect clarity. Almost as serene and clear as I had been beneath my tree. I slowly paced back to the Oxy-deck. I picked up my vodka bottle that had been sitting by my tree for as long as I had. *Apparently not for very long at all.* I took a long sip and poured the rest out for my tree. I noticed more leaves drying up and falling. I tore out a length of cable from a wall panel and tied the best slip knot I could. I began to climb, safe in the knowledge that the tree and I would be together forever, once again...

The Bizarchives

Stranger in the Morgue
by Marc Andre Chevalier

The spleen slipped out of Dr. Heinrich's trembling hands and fell off the autopsy table with a strange squishing sound. It glided across the linoleum floor, spinning furiously like a fallen ice skater after a botched Salchow.

"Ichenzee spracht!" Dr. Heinrich cursed.

At least I thought it was a curse, but my German was a little rusty. And even if I did understand German, he tended to mumble.

"Frank," he called. "Zee if you can find zat spleen!"

"OK doc, I'll find it…just don't move," I replied.

"Eh? Vat did you say?"

Rolling my eyes, I put the mop down and adjusted the visor on my biohazard suit. Doc's hearing was getting worse by the day, and judging from the flying gore, his Parkinsonian tremors weren't doing too well either.

"I SAID, 'DON'T WORRY, I'LL FIND THE SPLEEN.'"

He nodded and turned back to the cadaver.

I thought I noted a hint of gratitude in his eyes, but I couldn't see them too clearly through his Mr. Magoo glasses…and the "Mr. Magoo" part was no exaggeration. His coke-bottle spectacles - along with his bald head and prominent chin - made him a spitting image of the old cartoon character.

With another roll of my eyes, I started off across the morgue in dogged pursuit of the fugitive organ. The bloody trail led out of the dissection room, past the liquid nitrogen unit, and into Dr. Heinrich's office.

His desk had its usual appearance, with mounds of case files strewn around and scattered across the floor. The walls were lined by rusty filing cabinets, each with plumes of manila folders blossoming from open drawers.

Searching with a penlight, I finally found my quarry lodged between Heinrich's printer and a small doorstop shaped like a bust of Rudolf Virchow.

As I carried the spleen back, I reminded myself yet again how this job was only a temporary gig. I had never planned on being an autopsy technician (or, as my ID badge so eloquently stated, a "Forensic Custodial Technician"), but the pay was good, and the hours didn't interfere with my classes. Help with the autopsies. Clean up after crime scenes. No biggie.

Believe it or not, aside from dodging Dr. Heinrich's knife-wielding tremors, the job was pretty boring.

At least it had been until that very moment.

Just as I'd put the spleen back on the dissecting table, my cell phone rang.

It's no easy chore answering a cell phone in a blood-smeared moon suit, but I somehow managed to peel off the pants and dig around in my pocket before the caller hung up.

Annoyed, I hit the button.

"Frankie?" the voice said, with a hint of urgency.

"Yep. What's the problem, George?" I immediately recognized the rookie officer's squeaky voice.

"We need you in the Valley District. The detectives will be finishing up in a few minutes. You'd better prepare yourself…it's a doozy."

"Uh oh. What happened?"

"It looks like a domestic," he responded.

"Damn. Not another one."

"We got the call from a neighbor," George continued. "She heard screams and came over to see what was up. When she saw the body through the window, she called us."

"Do we know the specifics?"

"Well, there was a struggle," George said. "The kitchen is trashed, and a lot of furniture is broken. It looks like the assailant shocked him with a taser gun and then beat his brains out with a croquet mallet."

"Sheesh…and you think it's a domestic?" My opinion of marriage was pretty low, but that seemed a little excessive. "What did he do to his old lady that set her off like that?" I asked.

"Well," George replied with a chuckle. "We've heard some rumors that he cleaned out the family's bank account and blew it on jewelry for his mistress, after which he promptly filed for divorce. We can't be positive yet, but everything is pointing to his wife."

"Ahh…the old 'stash the bucks with the new doll' maneuver. Very clever, except that he didn't count on her temper."

"Anyhow," he said, "we need you to pick up the evidence bags. And the scene is pretty ugly too, so you'd better bring the heavy-duty mops."

"That's just ducky," I whined. "I'll be there in a few."

After relaying the situation to Dr. Heinrich, I packed my gear into the coroner's van and headed out to the site.

I pulled up to the house about twenty minutes later, just in time to see the detectives leaving the crime scene. The place looked like a real shithole. The ramshackle brick duplex had a crumbling porch and several broken windows. A plastic pink flamingo stood guard over waist-high piles of trash in the driveway, and a rusted-out 1983 Yugo sat up on cinder blocks in the front yard.

Resigned to my fate, I hopped out and went around back to unload the van. While I donned my gear, I spotted George loitering on the porch trying to look important in his new uniform. His peach-fuzz beard and pimply complexion made him look like a teenager at a Halloween party.

"Thank God you're here," he squeaked.

"They need to up your doughnut ration," I observed, "because you're still not filling out those blues."

He ignored my barb and grabbed my sleeve with a hint of panic in his eyes. "You aren't going to believe this one, Frankie," he said. "Come on up and I'll show you."

I grabbed my toolbox and followed him up the stairs. We weaved our way through a maze of rusted Yugo parts and eventually made it to the front door. Stepping into the foyer, I was immediately hit by the stench of dried blood.

George attempted to sound professional while he described the findings. "As you can see," he started, "there was

78

a scuffle in the living room."

Pieces of a coffee table lay scattered across the carpet and the walls were spattered with blood. Several lamps had been smashed on the floor.

"Calling it a 'scuffle' is a bit of an understatement, George," I said.

He merely shrugged in response.

As I scanned the room, I got a funny feeling that something wasn't right. "Wait a minute. Didn't you say that he was shocked and then bludgeoned?"

George frowned, not comprehending my point.

"Neither of those weapons should have caused this kind of spattering," I said.

He shook his head. "Oh…didn't I tell you about his chemo port?"

"What?"

"Yeah," he continued. "He was diagnosed with lung cancer last year. He had one of those injection ports for chemotherapy inserted into his chest. I guess the croquet mallet must have knocked it loose."

"You mean to tell me that this old guy was juggling a wife *and* a mistress while he was on chemo? It says on the paperwork that he was 75 years old!"

George turned and motioned me into the kitchen with another shrug.

It was a war zone. The microwave lay in tatters on the countertop, where it had been hurled during the melee. Several cabinet doors sagged drunkenly off their hinges. The toaster twirled in mid-air, hanging from an electrical cord tangled in the blades of the still-rotating ceiling fan. The cadaver lay sprawled on a small carpet next to the kitchen sink. He was a scrawny old man with thinning gray hair and a prominent, hawkish nose. He wore only a long, white bathrobe and a pair of fluffy slippers. His chemo port swung rhythmically from the left side of his chest wall, dripping pink fluid down his side. His entire forehead was caved-in by repeated impacts from the croquet mallet.

I looked over at George. "You might as well clear out and let me get to work. This could take a while."

George nodded and sauntered back to the porch for a cigarette.

I carefully collected all the evidence baggies onto a tarp and then started cleaning up. I had just zipped the remains into a body bag and was about to start mopping the floor when something caught my eye.

I moved closer to get a better look.

On the counter-top, a six-pack of malt liquor sat beside an open bag of pork rinds. Tense beads of a translucent, gelatinous substance clung to the sides of the cans. Strangely, whenever I looked directly at the drops, they *disappeared...* like some sort of optical illusion. Yet when I focused off to the side and used my peripheral vision, the drops came clearly into view. They had a consistency somewhere between bubble gum and toothpaste, and on careful examination, I noted a faint, green hue.

While examining the stuff, I also noticed it was slowly evaporating.

Once my eyes had become adjusted, I spotted more drops scattered all around the crime scene. A few had been splashed across the front of the dishwasher. Some were sprinkled on the body. I even noticed a drop on an old pizza box propped in the corner.

Unsure what it was, I ran outside for my toolbox. Unfortunately, by the time I found a bag and returned, the material had completely disappeared. I couldn't find a single drop anywhere; it had all evaporated.

Since I didn't want to sound crazy - and I had no idea what it was anyway - I decided I'd mention it to Heinrich later. I rounded up the evidence bags, tossed them into the van, and went to get George.

I found him hanging out in the driveway studying the flamingo. We picked up the body and hauled it to the front porch. Once we got it strapped onto the gurney, we zigzagged through the Yugo junk and hoisted it into the van. I'd just put my toolbox away when George stuck his head through the passenger window.

"Hey, Frankie...one more thing," he squeaked. "His mistress has been asking about a piece of jewelry. Supposedly, she gave him a ring, a band made of white gold. She wants it back. We've looked all over, and we can't find it. If you come across it somewhere, let us know."

It wasn't an unusual request, so I nodded and pulled away with a wave.

Truthfully, the whole "droplet" issue quickly faded from my mind. I wrote it off as nothing more than a strange fluke.

That is, until the "party".

About a week after the Yugo murder, I was hanging out in the morgue working the night shift. Things were quiet, so I kicked back in Heinrich's office for a few games of solitaire. I'd just cleared the junk from around his computer when my cell phone went off.

"Frankie?" George screeched.

"Yep, what's up?"

"We need you over in Glendale. It's a strange one."

"So we're going upscale this time?" I quipped. "What happened?"

"Just come over. I can't do it justice over the phone."

Intrigued, I rounded up my gear and headed out.

A half hour later, I pulled up to an ornate, Tudor mansion in the most exclusive part of town. Several detectives and a couple of TV cameramen milled about in the front yard. I spotted George standing on the front porch, trying to look busy.

He immediately spotted the van and came over.

"Put on your moon suit, Frankie," he said.

"Are you gonna tell me what's going on, or are you planning on keeping me in suspense all night?"

"Just follow me," he replied as I donned my gear.

We weaved through the camera crews and had just made it onto the porch when he decided to give me the low-down. "This place belongs to Jimmy Lee Birnbaum. You've probably seen him on the TV commercials."

I chuckled through the visor of my moon suit. "You mean the attorney...the injury-accident guy?"

"Yep." George waved his arms around dramatically. "This is some place, eh? It's unbelievable what a few years of ambulance-chasing can get you these days."

We stepped inside the foyer, and George motioned me into the front living room. Tiffany lamps, mahogany floorboards, and a gilded fireplace screen were the first things that jumped out at me.

"Not a bad spread, George. I should go to law school," I said.

"Nah," he replied. "Apparently, Birnbaum thought it was pretty boring, so he decided to take up a few hobbies." He pointed to the opposite side of the room.

Several large tables stood in the far corner, each holding a carefully arranged assortment of top-shelf S&M gear. I noticed the usual stuff…handcuffs, gag balls, and leather riding crops. The next table had a mundane assortment of creams, gels and dietary supplements.

But the last table had the really weird shit.

George picked up a strange gizmo that sprouted electrical wires and brass clips. "What do you suppose this is for, Frankie?"

I ignored him and took a careful look around. "What was going on in here?"

George took a sip of his coffee. "Well, as I understand it, he moonlighted as a rep for a sex-toy company. He was preparing for a large group of customers, sort of like an X-rated Tupperware party. One of the guests arrived a little early and found him stiff and cold."

"Where's the body?"

George motioned for me to follow. We went down a short hallway and into the dining room. A crystal chandelier swayed gently overhead in the draft of the furnace vent. In the center of the room stood a large oak table with trays of finger foods spread out on top. Several plates had been overturned, scattering small sausages and cheese assortments across the hardwood floor.

A corpse sat at the table, slumped face-down in a platter of deviled eggs. He wore only an orange leather thong, black lace stockings, and an extremely expensive pair of Italian high-heeled shoes. A stainless-steel fondue fork protruded from an ugly wound just below his right shoulder blade.

George clapped me on the back and headed outside to watch the reporters. "I'll leave this to you, Frankie."

I was going through my routine sweep and had just finished putting the last evidence baggies in my box…when I froze.

The green goop.

For a second, I hoped that it was just my imagination playing tricks, but in my heart, I knew.

I eased slowly over to the table and took a sideways look at a bottle of 1964 Sylvain-Cathiard sitting between two trays of stuffed mushrooms. Sure enough, there were several large globs of green gel clinging to the label.

Once I'd spotted the first few drops, I began seeing them everywhere. They dripped from the handle of the fondue fork. They were spattered across the chandelier. Some had pooled on the floor beneath the body.

Immediately, I rushed back into the living room. At first, I didn't see any. But after my eyes adjusted, I saw a few drops on the toy table. Then, I noticed a splatter on the fireplace screen.

Shit…the stuff was everywhere.

This time, I happened to have an evidence baggie in my back pocket. I found a large glob on the leather couch next to the fireplace. Very carefully, I scooped some of it with a sterile knife and sealed it inside.

I decided I'd show it to Dr. Heinrich when I got back. In the meantime, I kept quiet and finished my job.

Just when I'd loaded the body into the van, George waved at me from the lawn. Dashing through the snow, he skidded to a stop and knocked on the passenger window.

"Frankie," he said. "Did you happen to see any jewelry on the body?"

With a glance at the valuables container, I saw it was empty. "Nope. Sorry. I didn't find anything."

George frowned. "They tell me he had a pierced navel. One of the other toy reps says he loaned him a piece of demo jewelry to wear tonight...it plays Christmas music or something. He says it's made of white gold cast in the shape of holly leaves. They would like to have it back if you find it."

I freaked out.

White gold...again!

Green goo...again!

What in the world was going on?

I kept my composure and told George I'd keep an eye out for it.

When I finally pulled up to the coroner's office, I dashed inside and raced down to the morgue. Just as I approached Heinrich's office, I pulled the baggie out and took a quick look.

It had evaporated without a trace.

Stunned, I took the bag over to the dissection table and examined it under the swivel light, the one with a magnifying glass.

No luck.

Could it be a coincidence that both murders involved disappearing white gold jewelry and this strange material?

It hardly seemed possible. Yet without a sample to study, I couldn't really go any further.

After thinking the situation over, I decided once more to let it rest. I still had nothing but strange tales and unsubstantiated suspicions.

The next few days got even freakier. Now that I'd become aware of the *modus operandi,* I started seeing it over and over.

While the routine crimes never had the strange material, I noticed a specific set of killings that each had the same three findings: They were extremely brutal, they involved missing white gold jewelry, and the murder scene was always contaminated with the green goop.

The next incident was a gruesome killing at Daisy's Greenhouse in Melville. I arrived on scene to find Daisy's decapitated body slumped over a crate of mangoes. We searched for hours, finally discovering her head stuffed in a bag of Miracle-Gro over in the petunia section.

Green goop? Spattered all over her body and sprinkled across the flowers.

White gold anniversary necklace? Gone.

Two days later, we got a call about a case over in Erie Hills. An elderly farmer had been bludgeoned with a hoe and tossed into a manure spreader. I spent three hours cleaning up his remains with tweezers and a putty knife.

Green gel? Splashed all over the tractor.

White gold wedding ring? Gone.

Each time, I tried to collect a sample…and each time it evaporated before I could get it back to the lab. I tried airtight Ziploc bags. I tried plastic kitchenware. I tried latex balloons.

Nothing worked.

Whatever the stuff was, it disappeared rapidly and easily escaped air-tight containers.

So I decided to lay low and wait for a break. Sooner or later, even the most ingenious criminals make mistakes. It was only a matter of time.

About a week after the manure killing, I was in Heinrich's office goofing around on Minecraft when my cell phone went off.

"Frankie!"

It was George.

"What's up?" I asked.

"We need you over at the hockey rink. One of the coaches just turned up dead."

"OK, I'll be right over," I sighed.

I saved my work, packed up my gear, and headed out.

When I arrived, police were swarming all over. George looked nervous as he came over to the van. "This time, the killer was caught in the act," he said while trying to catch his breath.

"What happened?"

"Well," he continued, "the high school team had just finished practice and the players went home. The coach stayed behind to do some paperwork. About fifteen minutes later, three players came back to fetch a book bag they'd left in the locker room. When they came inside, they spotted a tall figure bludgeoning the coach with a goalie stick."

"Did they get a good look at the guy?"

"Unfortunately, no. The dome lights were all turned off. They said he was around seven feet tall and moved like greased lightning, but they could only see his profile."

"Seven feet tall! Geesh. Did he see the boys?"

"Yep. He tossed the hockey stick and ran across the rink. The guys said he slowed down when he hit the ice, so they took off after him. But when they got to the other side of the rink, he'd disappeared."

"I assume that you've searched the place?"

"Of course." George looked offended by the question. "We even have a few dogs inside right now. It looks like the killer escaped."

I gathered my stuff, zipped up my moon suit, and went inside.

The place looked like a madhouse. Cops, hockey players, and reporters were wandering everywhere. I called to one of the detectives and asked him to clear everyone away from the crime scene so I could collect the evidence. He nodded and had his men move everyone to the doors.

George led me over to the office where the coach's body had been found. The victim's eyes stared blankly at the ceiling, and he still clung to a clipboard in his right hand. The assailant had smashed him in the head with a chalkboard and then beat him senseless with the goalie stick.

Right away, I spotted a few green globs on the body.

The struggle had obviously been violent. Streams of blood spattered the walls and pooled on the floor. The desk lay upside down next to the body, and one of the windows was shattered.

It took me over an hour to collect the evidence and load it into the van. I'd just finished strapping the coach onto a gurney when George called to me from the ice.

I looked over in time to see him gingerly step out of the rink and make a beeline in my direction. He carried a small evidence bag in one hand and a couple of backpacks in the other.

"Frank. You'd better take these with you too. We found the player's book bag in the dressing room, and we found another one on the other side of the rink."

"The perp ran that way, didn't he?" I asked.

"Yep. None of the boys have ever seen this one. It's empty, but I'm wondering if it was dropped by the assailant."

I looked at the green bag in his hand and shrugged. "Well, I'll take it back to the lab and see if we can find anything."

George tossed both backpacks next to my gear.

"Oh, and you should take this too," he said. He waved the small evidence bag. "It's a necklace…white gold. The coach's wife says she gave it to him last Christmas. We found it out on the ice. It looks like the perp dropped it as he fled the scene."

My eyes went wide. I took the bag from George and examined it closely. Sure enough, it contained a small chain made of white gold.

The assailant didn't get away with his swag this time.

I quickly finished up and hopped into the van.

I arrived back at the coroner's office about an hour later, cautiously optimistic. But after a few minutes in the lab, my optimism soured.

Of course, the green gel I'd collected had long since evaporated. Of course, there were no fingerprints anywhere on the hockey stick. And of course, I found no physical evidence on either book bag or on the jewelry.

Seemingly, I'd hit another dead end.

At least, that's what I thought.

I was in Dr. Heinrich's office, staring dejectedly at the white gold necklace, when I heard a strange noise coming from the evidence vault. The muffled squeal sounded like someone trying to strangle a hamster.

Alarmed, I grabbed my keys and ran over to the vault. After a few seconds of fumbling, I managed to open the door and flip on the light.

Right there in front of my eyes I saw something stranger than anything I'd ever imagined. The green book bag was rolling around on the floor, shaking violently. *Slowly at first, the bag began to expand and take on a different shape!* It burst through the plastic evidence bag and kept right on growing.

I stood there, staring in stunned disbelief, as the thing began to take on a vaguely human shape.

After another minute, the thing stopped squealing, obviously finished with its metamorphosis. It stood almost seven feet tall and was made of a green, viscous material. It had two arms, two legs, and a big head that sloped awkwardly to the right. Its beady eyes flashed with an angry, hateful glare and its mouth was frozen into an ugly smirk.

Its gaze was fixed on the necklace I still held in my hand.

Immediately, it lunged at me.

I dashed across the lab and ran into the dissection room with the thing hot on my trail. It let loose a loud, angry squeal while it chased me in circles around the autopsy table.

Finally, it stopped and looked around the room, obviously searching for a weapon.

By this time, I'd gotten over my shock and was starting to get a little irate. After all, I'd survived some pretty nasty episodes back in my old neighborhood, and I could street fight with the best of them. I grabbed an empty Smirnov bottle that

I'd found on a dead vagrant the night before and smashed it against the wall.

"So you want a piece of Frankie Castellano?" I screamed while waving the jagged bottle at him. "Then come and get some, rubber-boy!"

That really pissed him off.

With a loud screech, he lunged over the table. I slashed him with the bottle, but the glass went right through his gooey arm.

The thing was strong, quick, and fought dirty. As I back-pedaled towards the histology lab, it picked up a ceramic urn and hurled it at me. I dodged to the side just as it smashed against the wall.

Seeing it was filled with ashes, the thing shattered another urn, scooped up a handful and threw it in my face.

Luckily, I was still wearing my safety goggles.

The thing screeched again and picked up a bone saw from the dissection tray. With a series of feints and shuffles, it maneuvered me into the corner.

With no way of escape, the situation was starting to look grim. It approached menacingly, and I'd started mumbling a prayer when a loud hissing sound rang out across the lab.

The thing froze and its skin began changing to a pale, whitish color.

Huddled in the corner, hands covering my face, I waited for the strike that never came. Eventually, I realized that the thing couldn't move. It stood there, sneer and all, lifeless as a statue.

"Ichenzee spracht!" Dr. Heinrich cursed.

I breathed a sigh of relief.

Mr. Magoo shuffled out from the shadows holding the hose from the liquid nitrogen tank.

"Zat was un close one," he quipped.

With his waddling, Parkinsonian gait, he shuffled over to get a better look at the thing.

I shook my head in disbelief. "What the hell is it?"

He lifted his Magoo lenses and stared at its face. "Un changeling...evil shape-shifter...der big green one, ya?"

"What...what the hell is a *changeling*?" I stood up and looked myself over. Luckily, I wasn't injured.

"Zey are evil beings zat kill for treasure. Za orange ones prefer diamonds, za blue ones crave silver. Der green ones kill for za white gold. We have zem everywhere in Eastern Europe...common pests, zey are. I vas vundering when it vould attack...been tracking it for months."

"You knew about this thing?" I gasped.

"But of course! Did you not see der green plasma at za crime scenes?"

"Uh...as a matter of fact, I did. I spotted it a couple weeks ago...but you've known about it for *months*?"

"Ya, ya," he said with a dismissive wave.

"Well thanks for the warning, asshole."

He gave a hearty laugh. "You Amerikaners...you do not *observe* your surroundings! You are too busy with der *video games* and der *reality shows*. You do not pay attention to vat is going on around you! Your analytical faculties have atrophied! *You do not believe anything zat is not right in front of za nose!*"

He turned his attention back to the shape-changer. "Za nitrogen froze its plasma. It vill slowly melt and evaporate."

92

Right then and there, I quit.

It was only a temporary gig, and I had no intention of getting whacked by some Gumby-on-steroids just to earn tuition money.

After a few weeks, I found another job as a night watchman at an auto dealership. Compared to what I'd seen back at the coroner's office, it was a nice change. All I had to do was hang out in the guard hut and watch TV.

But I don't think I'll ever get the experience totally out of my head. To this day, I still have nightmares. Sometimes, when I'm watching the evening news, they'll show footage of a murder scene. Before I can stop myself, I slide up to the TV and press my face against the screen.

Most of the time, nothing is there.

But every once in a while, I see it. Sometimes the goop is orange...sometimes it's blue...and sometimes it's from a green one.

I try not to think about it. I've never told anyone what happened until now...but people should know the truth.

As God as my witness, they're out there...and they could strike at any time.

Avenger of the Oil
by Greg Kay

It was half-past midnight. Elvis was playing a blues duet with Louis Armstrong, James Dean was mixing a dry martini behind the bar, and Humphrey Bogart was talking trash to a fifty-year-old fat woman at a corner table. It was just another evening at Sal Rosenberg's Club Noir.

Outside, the rain looked like it had settled in for the duration, but instead of washing the dirty pavement clean, it just made it stink like the river on a hot day. Inside, the stink was different; you couldn't smell the rain, but there was still a definite odor about the place that overrode the smells of smoke and spilled booze that curled like ghosts through the stale air of the dimly lit bar. My nose is sensitive, and the last time I smelled anything like that was at an old people's home where the aged, confined to their beds, had nothing more to look forward to than dying. It stank of misery and quiet despair.

They call me Jack Diamond. I was parked at my usual table nursing a shot of scotch when Marilyn Monroe came by with her cigarette tray.

"Cigarette? Cigar?" she breathed, or maybe purred in the way only Norma Jean could, leaning over so far she threatened to break out of her low-cut red dress and send her substantial assets spilling out onto the table. Before reaching for a pack of Camels, I scooted my drink over a little, just in case.

I opened the pack and stuck one between my lips, and she took a lighter from her tray and flipped it open for me.

"Didn't anyone ever tell you that stuff's bad for you?" she asked as she lit me up.

I took a deep drag and smiled, being careful not to get ashes on my best dark suit, and put the money on her tray.

"Life's what's bad for you, honey; kills us all in the end."

Her laugh was a musical tinkle with all the humor of a shattering champagne glass.

"Ain't that the truth, Jack?" she said, and then repeated it with the faintest trace of sadness in her voice that only someone like me could hear, "Ain't that the truth?"

I watched her walk away, the normally sinuous sway of that gorgeous backside marred by an almost imperceptible limp that was centered in the mechanical joint of her left hip. It must have been another rough customer, and her cheapskate boss hadn't even bothered to have her repaired. Sal was never one to take good care of his equipment, which was why I was here to work a deal with him.

You might say I'm a repairman; I fix things that don't work like they should.

Looking around, I could see that none of the other celeb-bots here were in tip-top shape either. Most people – particularly the kind of low-lifes who frequented dives like this one – would never notice, but then again, most people weren't me. James Dean, for instance, favored his right arm just a bit as he shook the ice and gin behind the bar, from a worn Teflon joint long past the need for replacement, unless I missed my guess. Elvis and Louis looked like they both had more than a little hitch in their git-along too, and the bouncers, Errol Flynn and John Wayne, were carrying battle scars that a little bit of silicone and a trip to the paint shop would have fixed right up.

Shaking my head, I looked into my drink like the answer might be there. The bots – the celeb-bots in particular, which were high-end models – given a little TLC, were damned near indestructible...not that people didn't try, of course.

All the bots in Club Noir were there solely for the pleasure of the customers. Any pleasure at all, as long as you had the cash. You could do things to bags of silicone on titanium and polymer frames who looked, talked, and acted like important people with no social implications at all: things that would land you in divorce court or the big house for some hard time if you even thought about doing them to a human being. Even the people they were made to duplicate couldn't complain; they were all long dead.

The customers who frequented places like this – theme bot-bars – could live out their fantasies in the rooms upstairs at the expense of machines they considered to be no more human than a vibrator with legs; a collection of sculpted synthetic material and circuits, with just enough cloned brain tissue wired in to make it react like a human being within a limited range. A little harmless fun; the bots had pressure sensors instead of nerves, and thus they couldn't actually feel pleasure or pain, despite the fact that the signals sent by the attempts to inflict either caused their hybrid brain to react as if they did, within the limits of their programming. All you could hurt was their dignity, and as machines, they had none. At least, that's what some people thought.

There were other people who thought differently, though. They claimed that the bots' systems were so detailed that pain was what they actually felt, and that, as the human parts of their brains matured, could not only begin to have independent thoughts but even emotions: love, hate, the whole works.

Maybe some people have big imaginations, too; then again, maybe not.

I was so deep in pondering the justice of it all that I didn't notice when Boris Karloff came up behind my chair and startled the hell out of me. He was always good at that, and the fact that he looked like an undertaker towering over me in his somber black suit didn't help.

"Mr. Rosenberg will see you now."

I left the half-finished drink on the table as I stood up and followed him. The crowd was thinning down, and we only brushed by a few people as we wound our way through the tables. Lauren Becall was sitting silently, staring off into space with a cigarette holder between her fingers, while her human companion was in the john. Like Marilyn, I had known her for a long time, but she didn't look up as I passed. I couldn't really blame her.

Boris stopped before a substantial oak door decorated with several unsavory and unidentifiable stains, three bullet holes, and a sign that said "PRIVATE." He rapped it with his knuckles. I grimaced as I heard the sound of the loose joints clacking inside his hand.

"It's Mr. Diamond to see you, sir."

There was a muffled voice from inside that sounded vaguely profane, and my guide opened the door, gesturing for me to enter. If I were not who I was, I might have shivered when it banged shut behind me, leaving me face to face with

Sal's bodyguard, a permanently shifty-looking Peter Lorre, with one hand thrust inside his double-breasted jacket.

I knew the drill, and unbuttoned my coat without being asked, then lifted the tails and turned in a three-sixty to show him I wasn't carrying. He took his hand off his gun, treated me to his trademark sick smile and servile nod, and stepped aside, leaving me face to face with his boss. That was not an improvement.

To say that Sal Rosenberg was an evil man would be to give evil a slanderously bad name. He sat there in his sagging swivel chair like a bloated spider crouching behind the cluttered desk, stinking of sweat and cigar smoke. Oily perspiration poured from his bald head, gathered in the corners of his piggy little eyes, and dripped from the tip of his big, veined nose. His multitude of chins flowed over his shirt collar, hiding the knot of his tie, and the greasy fat rolls bulged his ugly green and yellow striped suit, actually swallowing parts of it. Garish gold rings decorated every last, fat finger. The whole office – porno pictures on the walls and all – reeked of him. The big cigar stump that jutted from his wide, thick-lipped mouth like a half-completed bodily function was just the icing on the cake.

"Good evening, Mr. Rosenberg. Thanks for taking the time to see me."

"Cut the crap, Diamond, and tell me what you want. I'm a busy man." His voice was gravelly and hoarse from the cigars, and I wasn't surprised when he didn't invite me to sit down. From the looks of the filthy chair on my side of the desk, I'm sure I heard my suit breathe a sigh of relief.

"Very well, sir, I'll come right to the point. You've got bots here that need repair, and that's what my new firm does: fix whatever's wrong with bots. We do a thorough job, and our rates are very reasonable."

"Are you tryin' to run a scam on me? My bots are fine for what I need 'em for."

"I can make them better."

"I don't need 'em better, and therefore we got nothin' to discuss." He turned to sneaky Pete. "Show this peddler to the door!"

"Yes, Mr. Rosenberg," he simpered in his drawn-out way, and reached out for my arm. "Make it easy on yourself, Diamond."

I took his advice and did just that. I abruptly grabbed his hand; the two sharp probes blasted outwards through my palm and in through the insulating synthetic layers of his skin. They kept going until they touched metallic bone and sent a couple of hundred thousand volts of electricity blasting through his system, scrambling his circuits and dropping him in a convulsing heap on the floor.

I'll say this for Sal; he was fast for a big man. He had come up from the streets the hard way, and he still had his instincts. He had the desk drawer open and almost had his right hand on his pistol when my own hand closed around his thick wrist…and squeezed.

Sal's face ran through a whole chorus line of expressions from anger to shock to disbelief to agonizing pain as my artificial fingers closed, first breaking, then crushing his wrist bones, and then pulping the flesh. I'll never forget that little "O" his mouth made when I squeezed his hand all the way off and dropped it in his lap. There was surprisingly little blood, since the force had pinched the arteries together, leaving the ragged stump no more than seeping.

Sal looked at me accusingly, his face an even more sickly

pale green than usual.

"You – you're a bot!"

I took the smoldering butt from between my lips and casually dropped it, crushing it into the carpet with my heel.

"You're a smart boy, Sal; got it in one," I told him as I reached for his left hand, smiling all the while. "You might say I'm an advanced model."

It was fifteen minutes before I left the office and closed the door behind me. I brushed off my sleeves and straightened my lapels before walking back out in the barroom and motioning for Marilyn.

"You need another pack to go, Jack?"

"No," I told her as I took the strap from around her neck and set the tray on the nearest table. "I need you to go. Come on, Baby; you're taking the evening off. Let's blow this joint."

"But Mr. Rosenberg…"

"I don't think you'll have to worry about complaints from him. I fixed it."

She glanced at the office door before I hooked her arm through mine and started walking. We stopped long enough at the hatcheck desk to collect my fedora and trench coat from Betty Grable, and we walked out the front door into the night.

The rain had stopped, and, while the place still smelled, at least the stars were starting to come out.

Grim and Serpent
by William Gable

Grim had once been a Viking and a powerful warrior, but now he found himself in a curious situation. After his glorious death on the battlefield, he had awoken, much to his dismay, not in the golden halls of Valhalla, but in a strange new world. His memories were fragmented and in a fog, or some kind of magical amnesia. He could only summon up faint shadows of who he once was. The only clues to his new purpose he had received were in a cryptic message, delivered by a talking raven. By Odin's decree, if he wanted to join his battle brothers, he must slay the five wayward Jotun that had been banished to this realm.

In spite of his amnesia, Grim felt he was a capable warrior. He could recall glimmers of past victories, heroic adventures, wild drunken parties, and hours planning and preparing for battle. However, dealing with Jotun was something he was pretty sure he'd never before attempted. He knew that he was going to need tools for battle. To this end, he had employed all of his resourcefulness to prepare for these future encounters. In past weeks, he had explored his surroundings and discovered that he was stranded on a small temperate island. Food was easy enough to come by; wild berry bushes and edible mushrooms seemed to grow everywhere. On several occasions, he spied deer and wild pigs roaming the woodlands of the isle. Once he had fashioned himself a stone tipped hunting spear, game was easy to take.

However, there were many dangers about this place that Grim had yet to learn. His first night on this strange and magical island almost spelled his doom. When darkness fell, the woods came to life, literally. Moss, vines, roots, branches and stones cobbled themselves together in the failing light. Bipedal aberrations with glowing eyes beset Grim. And he only just escaped their wrath with quick reflexes and the use of a flaming branch from his camp fire. The next day, after a full night of battling these fey creatures, he resolved to build himself some kind of fortified encampment.

Before long, Grim had himself a stout hut, complete with thatched roof and a stone and clay fireplace, as well as a roomy, fenced yard in a green meadow a short walk from a beach. During the day, he would scavenge, hunt, fish, and explore. At night, he would stoke a large fire at his camp and bar the door of his hut. This seemed to do well enough keeping the creatures at bay. During his explorations, he marveled to find veins of native copper and tin protruding from rock outcroppings around the island. Memories of working metal came to him. With some ingenuity, he gathered the metals and set to crafting himself tools and weapons of copper and bronze. In short order, he had added a workshop to his encampment and was feeling pretty proud of his accomplishments. It was then that Grim learned another hard lesson.

Out on the sea, Grim had ridden a small raft to try his luck at catching some fish. He was distracted with a tangled line and watching the sky for the incoming storm and did not see the creature approach. With a hollow thud, Grim's raft bucked violently sideways. He lost his balance and stumbled off into the cold waters.

Grim gasped for breath when he resurfaced and flailed for a grip on the side of the raft. Out of the corner of his eye, he caught a flash of movement below the surface: slithering metallic green and black scales against the bottomless abyss below. He grasped for the edge of the raft and attempted to hoist himself up but was pulled below by a sharp tug on his trouser leg. In the blur of the underwater and swirling bubbles, he could make out a green glowing eye and a maw of teeth gripping his pant leg. In a panic, he swung his fist down, striking the eye. This must have startled the creature, because it reflexively released his leg and snapped at his arm. The teeth dug deep into his flesh momentarily but then released. Grim frantically swam for the surface. With fight or flight response in overdrive, he grabbed the edge of the raft and vaulted onto the deck.

By now, the storm had arrived. Wind wiped over the waters, creating huge swells. Rain poured from the sky, blowing sideways. Ignoring the pain in his arm, Grim looked for shore and saw that it wasn't far off. The wind was in his favor. He lowered the raft's improvised sail, and gusts of wind launched the small craft forward. His arm began throbbing with stabbing pain. Looking down at it, he could see a row of at least a dozen puncture wounds, and blood was oozing freely from his injuries. He ripped the sleeve from his tunic and began tightly wrapping his arm to slow the bleeding.

He was suddenly jarred as the raft was struck again. It bucked sideways and he was nearly thrown from it once more. The creature was still after him. Fearfully looking over the edge of the raft, he could see in the fading light that it was some kind of monstrous serpent. Greenish black scales, glowing green eyes, webbed dorsal fins, and gaping jaws filled with menacing fangs launched at the raft. When the jaws clamped down on the raft, Grim leaped into action, drawing his knife and driving it down hard on the creature's head. The blade struck one of the heavy green plated scales and glanced away harmlessly. The serpent, jaws clamped tight, began to thrash and shake violently. Within seconds Grim was thrown overboard again as the little craft came apart from this final assault.

All he could do now was swim for shore. He swam with all of his might. Luck was with Grim. In less than a minute, he was staggering up the beach. Between the rough waters, the fragments of raft, and his proximity to land, he had eluded the hunter. Looking over his shoulder, he could just make out the serpent coiling around and through the wreckage of his raft still searching for him. It would seem that the creature had no interest in coming to shore. Within a few more minutes, it disappeared back into the depths.

Grim staggered through the rain back to the safety of his camp. He narrowly avoided another encounter with more of those forest fey creatures as they began to materialize and let out a sigh as he latched the door of his hut. He set to work right away treating his injury. He cleaned his arm, coated it with some honey he had collected, and wrapped it with cloth. This was going to take some time to heal, but he didn't fear it was a mortal wound. After stoking up his fire, he crawled into his bed. As he drifted to sleep, he began planning his revenge. It would be a few weeks' worth of preparations before the day would come when Grim was ready.

Golden rays of sunlight danced between the oak and beech leaves, dappling rich green grass as Grim worked the finishing touches on his latest creation. With a grunt of satisfaction, he looked over his newly constructed fishing harpoon: a sturdy wooden haft, the business end bristling with barbed and jagged pearly shell fragments he had harvested a day earlier. It was all fastened together tightly with tough leather and sinew and trailed with a long, hand-woven rope.

"This ought to do the trick," he said to himself, thrusting with the weapon. He was ready to find the serpent that tried to take his life, and repay in kind.

Turning and entering his modest wood and thatch hut, he gathered up all of the supplies he thought he would need for this adventure. Into his open knapsack, he dropped some dried meat, a couple of torches, flint and striker, a full water skin, and a small hunting knife. He then donned his protective armor. Polished bronze plates riveted onto a leather vest, a simple helm with a nasal guard and a set of bronze bracers made up his kit.

Grim thought to himself, "This probably won't protect me from the full force of a bite, but it's better than nothing. I just hope I don't end up going for a swim."

Slinging the knapsack over his shoulders, he reached for the final compliment to his attire, a glistening bronze battle axe hanging over his hearth. Tucking the axe into his belt, he propped the harpoon over his shoulder and headed out. Exiting the dwelling, he took the well-trod path, winding through the woods, down to the beach.

Grim arrived at the shore line and shrugged off his knapsack into the boat. Among his activities of the past weeks, he had built himself a fine small karve. He knew it would be foolish to go out to sea again in a craft that was slow or lacked maneuverability. This boat was lightweight, swift, stable and easy to control. He shoved out to sea, lowered his sails and began swiftly gliding over the waters. It was mid-day with clear skies, but Grim knew by now that the weather could change rapidly.

As he scanned the waters, he also watched the island shrink into the distance. He didn't know how far he would have to go, and he really didn't want to lose sight of shore, but he figured if the creature was still out there, he may have to cover a lot of distance to find it. The day wore on, and the sun was getting low on the horizon when Grim decided to start making his way back towards land. The wind had changed direction, and he could see a storm quickly approaching.

Grim was digging into his knapsack to feast on some dry meat when a heavy gust of wind caught his sail and rocked the boat hard to port. He withdrew and lit a torch as the sky darkened with clouds and a gentle rain began to fall. Soon the ocean began to toss with large swells as the wind grew stronger. Grim aimed the prow of the boat in the direction he knew his land should be, as thunder and lightning cracked the sky. A feeling of excitement washed over him as the storm grew more intense. Despite the rocking of the waves and the now pouring rain, Grim had steely focus on the seas around him.

"The hunter becomes the hunted," he thought to himself.

Grim peered over the side of his ship, lit torch still in hand. The waters beneath were a black abyss. He could see nothing there, but he felt it in his gut that the time was near. Then it happened. Off the port bow, only a few yards from his ship, the head of the serpent breached the waters. Grim watched in amazement as the creature reared up out of the sea, taller than his mast, and let out a bellowing roar as his boat glided past. In a flash, Grim had the harpoon in hand and aimed for the creature's underbelly. He knew that top scales were hard, nearly impenetrable, but maybe it would have a softer underside. He aimed and let loose his projectile. It soared through the darkness, rain, and wind and found its mark. The sharp barbs dug deep into the creature's flesh. Grim had secured the harpoon's lanyard to the ship's mast. The serpent recoiled from the attack and the rope snapped tight, jerking the boat, but everything held fast.

"Now I have you!" shouted Grim as he manned the rudder.

The serpent dove beneath the surface, and Grim could feel its might tugging the ship to and fro, but the line and mast still held fast. He looked over the horizon, and through the gloom of the storm could just make out what he thought was the shore. The boat rocked, and the wind howled. Grim fought the efforts of the monster. The boat would lurch one way then the other as the snake struggled. Then suddenly, the line went slack. For a moment, he cursed as he thought the creature had freed itself. He realized his mistake when the hull of the boat took a mighty slam. The serpent was attacking the ship. He jumped up from the rudder and drew his axe looking over the side. The coils of the creature could be seen turning against the hull. He swung his axe down at an opportune time and felt the blade bite into the flesh. The serpent replied with a whip of its tail. Grim ducked just in time, but the tail sent splintered fragments of wood flying in all directions as it damaged the hull some more.

Grim grabbed for the rope tied to the mast and began tugging at it violently. Maybe that would cause the snake to recoil again. It worked, almost too well. As the snake lurched away from the boat, He was nearly yanked overboard. He let the rope free and jumped to take the rudder again. He could see now that the shore was agonizingly close but the serpent had managed to redirect the boat, and the course had to be corrected.

The boat was filling with water now from all of the damage it sustained. Adding to that, the cresting waves, and driving rain, this craft would not stay afloat much longer. The snake was now pulling away from land with all its might, but the wind was still inching the ship closer and closer to salvation. Grim could see the lapping of the waves on the beach, it was so close. Again, the line suddenly went slack. Grim turned to look behind him and saw the beast's head, once again, rise up out of the water. It was coming down right on top of him for one more desperate attack. Thinking quickly, he sprang to his feet and rushed the mast. With one hand, he caught hold of the rope and in the other hand he used his axe to sever the knot securing the harpoon. Pivoting around the mast, he dodged the serpent's attack. Wide open jaws with rows of razor teeth slammed into the ship's deck as Grim leaped from the prow of the ship. He landed in the water, but found he was close enough to shore that it was only knee deep. Without looking back at the thrashing beast, he sprinted onto dry land, rope in hand, and found a sturdy stump. He pulled the slack from the rope and rapidly coiled it around the anchor. As he tied a hasty knot, the rope snapped tight as the beast tried to yank itself free once more.

Looking down past the waters edge, Grim could see the serpent squirming and wriggling against the rope. Its coils splashed and thrashed in the shallow water among the ruins of the ship. It let out hisses and howls of pain. Grim lowered his head. He fixed his gaze on the beast, tightened his grip on the axe, and in the dark beating rain, gravely marched down the line toward his foe.

There was a dim red glow barely visible on the western horizon, between the sea and clouds. Lightning and thunder cracked overhead, briefly illuminating Grim's opponent in flashes as it coiled and twisted in the foamy waters. The serpent was big. Bigger than Grim had imagined. He was unsure if he had the strength or the tools to dispatch such a beast. He glanced at the taunt, bounding rope that was anchoring the creature and, for a brief moment, considered severing the line, letting the danger return to sea.

"No," he said to himself, "if I don't finish this now, it will only come back to me again later. And maybe when I am in a worse position."

With axe in hand, Grim began his charge. He sprinted over the beach into the water, a swift, dark silhouette in the nearly absent light. As Grim came within striking distance, the serpent reared its head up. In a flash, Grim saw those glowing green eyes and rows of razor teeth coming down on him. He dove to his left, but a moment too late. The snake seized him about the abdomen in mid jump. He felt himself being lifted into the air as the jaws and fangs began to crush the breath out of him. He could feel his ribs near breaking under the pressure. But his armor was warding away the worst of the stabbing fangs. Both hands now gripping the axe, Grim swung the weapon with all of his might into the side of the serpent's head. The beast roared out in pain, releasing its grip, sending him falling. Grim could taste the spray of blood that had been released as he plummeted into the waters..

He was still in the shallows; the water broke his fall somewhat, and he was able to get his footing to stand in preparation for the next attack. The snake was now slithering along the ground, between him and the shore, cutting off any chance of escape. Its body was only half submerged by the knee-deep waters. Grim could see the snake was keeping its distance, perhaps a bit more reluctant now that it had taken injury. In a crack of thunder and lightning, the thick green, metallic, dorsal scales glistened, all facing his direction.

"It's on the defensive now," thought Grim.

He glanced down to his belt and took his hunting knife with his left hand. Grim knew he was in a tight spot now, and he was going to have to take some calculated risks. The creature's underbelly was the only place vulnerable enough for his weapon to pierce, so he was going to have to force that position.

He moved toward the creature's midsection. The serpent responded to this by coiling its head and tail around behind Grim, effectively encircling him. With an eye over his shoulder, he watched the head of the beast as he leaped over the serpent's body, an attempt to escape. He didn't see the attack coming. With a hard thwack, Grim briefly saw stars as his helm was knocked from his head. He went end-over-end and landed face up in the sand and surf.

"The damned tail," Grim realized far too late.

Grim was oriented with his feet pointing at the shore and his head toward the sea and serpent. As his double vision corrected itself, he could see the serpent once again rise up for another strike. He knew there would be no dodging this attack, but Grim now had another plan. Extending his left arm, he held the knife, blade down, as an easy and sacrificial target for the beast. The serpent took the bait, and its maw snapped around his arm. Grim could feel fangs dig into and pierce his bronze bracer and mar his flesh. But it was a far less egregious wound as it would have been unarmored. At the same time, he felt the blade of his knife bury deep into the roof of the beast's mouth.

With a hissing shriek, the snake released its bite on

Grim. He rolled and stood in one motion, then, using the momentum, took an upward arching sweep with his axe at the beasts throat. Thick, dark and tangy blood came pouring from the wound, covering Grim and splashing into the sea like a waterfall. The beast reared up and back as high as it could, simultaneously releasing a gurgled roar. The harpoon and rope which were still attached again went taunt, preventing the creature from retreating. Grim lurched forward for another mighty strike, burying his axe up to the handle in its underbelly. More fresh blood came pouring out from this new wound; maybe he had found its heart. The sea serpent then toppled over with a thud and splash as if it was a fallen tree.

Grim freed his axe and walked to the serpent's head. The once bright glowing eyes were now dim and weakening by the moment. With several chops, Grim separated the head from the beast. Its body now slowly twisted in the surf. Almost as if in perfect time with the creature's death, the rain subsided and the clouds began to break. Stars twinkled in the night sky.

Grim looked over the corpse of his foe and thought to himself, "I bet those scales would make a superb shield." It would be a lot of work to butcher and scavenge this beast, but Grim estimated it would be well worth his while.

A sound suddenly caught Grim's ear. Over the sound of the lapping waves, the snapping of twigs and the dull thud of rocks on moss could be heard from behind. He turned and looked to the woods just beyond the beach. In the darkness, dozens of glowing pairs of eyes moved in the treeline. The nighttime fay aberrations were mobilized, marching his way.

"Well," said Grim, feeling the weight of his axe, "I guess it's going to be another long night."

114

The Crypt of St. Peter's Church
by Robert C. Booth

The rain was pouring down heavily outside, and there were rumbles of thunder in the distance when I woke late in the afternoon. I should never have allowed Joseph to ply me with drink as he did. The whole night had become rather too boisterous for my liking.

I rolled over in bed to face the grandfather clock that was ticking away in the corner. It was a rather handsome thing with a mahogany case that was adorned with images of cherubim gathering over an image of an idyllic town. The clock face read half past two. It was much too late in the day to make getting dressed worthwhile, so I decided to spend the rest of the day idle.

Knock. Knock.

The door rattled with the hammering of the knocker.

"Who ever could that be?" I thought to myself. I had been excused from work ever since the Drughbury incident, so it

115

was unlikely to be Mr. Prendergast baying for my blood.

"Who is it?!" I shouted, my voice still hoarse from the night of inebriety.

"Mr. Bennet, Mr. Reuben Bennet?" The voice was heavy, deep, and panicked.

"Yes it is, who is calling?" I started to worry that a forgotten memory from the night before had returned to cause me trouble.

"Could you open the door please Mr. Bennet, it is urgent!" The voice replied anxiously, "It is I, Father Smethwick, Vicar of St. Peter's church. I require your assistance immediately!"

"Hold on Father, I will be but a moment." Still wearing my bedclothes, I cautiously approached the door to look through the gap along the door-frame.

An old white-haired man stood wearing a long black frock-coat with a tall white collar, he looked panicked and flustered.

"Ever so sorry to keep you, Father, whatever do you need me for?" I opened the door and the elderly priest grabbed my hand.

"You must help, there is no time to delay, you must get dressed and accompany me to the church as soon as you are able to."

"Give me one moment Father." I carefully extricated myself from his grip and closed the door. Whatever could he want?

I hurriedly found a white shirt and some black trousers to wear, put on my shoes, and picked up my smart dark grey coat off of the chair. I grabbed my silk cravat and, realising it may be needed, my revolver from the drawer, and I opened

116

the door again.

"We must hurry!" Father Smethwick shouted as he started down the stairs, and I made after him.

The streets of Totbrook were as they usually were on such a time of day: children playing alleys, tiggy-it, and whip and top, mothers gathering to speak news of the day and tradesmen moving between engagements.

"He was t'one that killed that thing." A woman called out as we turned the corner for St. Peter's. She was referring to my recent encounter with a Cyhyraeth on Drughbury Moor, a fey creature that portends death with her horrific wailing.

I still bore the marks of her unworldly influence. Ever since the encounter I had been having peculiar dreams of weird tales played out before my eyes, as if they were taken from some repository deep in my subconscious. In my drunken slumber I had seen dark walls and heard a strange voice, the clear memory of which now eluded me in my wakefulness.

"There is a girl in the crypt." The vicar's voice pulled me out of my thoughts as we faced the large stone church that took pride of place in the town square of Totbrook.

It more closely resembled a cathedral than a normal town church. It was built in a Gothic style with large stained glass windows and heavy arches. Above my head I could see a particularly grim gargoyle staring at me as I approached the broadly-arched doorway.

We made our way through the doors where a group of churchmen and assorted members of the laity were anxiously waiting for us. The sickly-sweet smell of incense struck me immediately; Father Smethwick was something of an Anglo-Catholic. The assembled party moved with excitement and without hesitation towards the priest.

"Father, will he help us?" A bestubbled old man at the head of our greeting party asked us anxiously.

"Why John, I do think he may be able to." Father Smethwick took a deep breath and turned to me, "Mr. Bennet, like I said, we have a girl in the crypt."

"I am sorry to hear that." I bowed my head as a token of respect.

"Oh no, she is not dead." Father Smethwick smiled briefly before returning his expression to solemnity.

"No, she is possessed by a demonic entity." His face betrayed no jest, and the group around him gave no giggle or murmur, he was serious.

"Possessed? Why then did you call for my aid?" I am sure my face must have betrayed my consternation.

"Mr. Bennet, I do not know how to say this, but the demon asked for you personally. Perhaps it heard of your encounter in Drughbury. I do not know, but there must be no more delay."

With that I was marched through the sanctuary and towards a small corridor, with the rest of the assembled churchmen following.

The smell of incense was even more pungent, I could only surmise that this was the thurifer's cut-through while undertaking his duties. The priest showed me to a backroom stairway.

"The girl is in the crypt, just through here. Her name is Mary James; she is a local girl and is known to dabble in all kinds of sorcery." The priest pointed down some more steps.

I apprehensively descended the staircase, the smell of incense growing ever stronger as I approached the bottom. The stone crypt's air was stagnant but for the sickly smell of
118

incense, which was burning from a metal censer at the bottom of the staircase. Candles flickered, scarcely lighting my way as I turned into the main chamber.

I heard a voice in a tongue that was unfamiliar and yet somehow intelligible. A young woman with jet black hair strewn across her face sat in the far corner of the room. Her dress was black and trimmed with lace, and she wore fine black boots. I noticed a silver pendant lay on the ground beside her, the chain broken. I approached her, my heart rate increasing with every step.

She looked at me wild-eyed, her striking brown eyes still visible through her thick black hair. I could only guess from her features (and surname) that she was of Welsh ancestry.

"Mary? Mary James?" I called. She continued speaking curious words as she stared into my eyes. I felt a fleeting pain in the same part of my mind that I had felt the Cyhyraeth burrowing into a week earlier.

"Mary James is not here!" Her chest heaved as a breathy male voice spoke through her.

"Then to whom am I speaking?!" I found myself foolishly fumbling towards my revolver.

"That infernal device can do me no harm, boy and fortunately for you I mean to do you none." A forced smile appeared on the girl's face, causing me an uneasy feeling.

"Leave the girl and go, Abomination!" I made towards the silver pendant.

"If you wish to know of the danger that surrounds your cousin Eleanour Townley, you shall listen!" The demon voice boomed.

"You will never lay your or anybody else's hands on Eleanour," I snarled through gritted teeth. The demon laughed with an inhuman croak.

"I am not here to threaten you or any other women you harbour an unspoken desire for Mr. Bennet. No, I am here to warn you." My face turned red at the baseless insinuation.

"I am not in love with-"

"Your pathetic attempt at denial hurts me more than your crude attempt upon my borrowed form, Mr. Bennet." The demon swept Mary James' hair from her face revealing an unusual looking but beautiful young woman.

"I came into possession of Miss James as her spirit was wandering through places she should not have wandered in, in search of your future tidings. I am here to present you with a warning, Mr. Bennet." The possessed girl stood up. Her exquisite dress draped well over her stout but ample form.

"She was scrying, much as her mother and generations of her grandmothers have done before her. She was scrying tea leaves for your cousin, that is when she saw it."

"When she saw what?" I asked.

"When Mary saw the impending danger currently winding its way towards you. She was hesitant to speak of what she saw to your cousin."

"And why is that?" I queried.

"Eleanour Townley, your cousin, will bring grave danger upon you." The demon stopped, silence hung upon the stale air of the crypt as my mind raced with the implications of the demon's words.

"You lie! You come to cast aspersions on my cousin and induce me to be fearful of her!" I cast my words upon Mary James' form as it began to rise from the ground with a jerking motion, as if she unfolded herself from the floor and pushed herself upwards in one clean movement.

120

The demon pointed at the silver pendant and with a scrape along the floor flicked the pendant towards me. I caught the silver bird-skull pendant with ease.

"If I speak a lie, then press the silver upon my form and cast me to the world outside of this reality!" The demon opened its arms and closed its eyes, willingly embracing banishment to the ether. I accepted that the demon must be, as far as such a being can be, well intentioned.

"Who are you?" I spoke to the being, who upon hearing my question smiled through Mary's lips.

"I have no name for myself in this realm. It is shrouded in the mists of wakefulness and the ignorance that it inevitably brings. You may, if you prefer, call me 'Tom Salt.'" The name dripped of some unknown irony I was not a party to. Nonetheless, I could sense earnestness in the creature.

"Assuming I do believe your warning, how can Eleanour, my dearest cousin, bring any harm upon me?" I asked.

"Misconstrue me not, Mr. Bennet. Eleanour means you no harm, but being near her shall invite your death!" The demon began jolting its acquired form wildly, limbs lengthening and contracting in an instant, its head shaking from side to side.

"What is happening?" I shouted at the being, "Tom Salt! What are you doing?".

"I… am…" The demon croaked again before it stopped jolting and Mary James collapsed to the floor in a heap.

At first I thought her dead, exhausted from Tom Salt's possession of her body, but suddenly Mary began breathing heavily and panicking so I rushed over to aid her.

"Who are you, where am I?" She asked me frantically as her heart thumped in her chest. I put my arm round her which soothed her somewhat

"You were possessed by a demon calling itself 'Tom Salt;' he warned me of danger, danger you foresaw in your tasseomancy." What I said was evidently a shock to her as she looked at me in both horror and recognition.

"Tom Salt is my spirit guide. He is no demon!" she said.

Mary regained her composure after several strong drinks. The Butcher's Arms was fairly busy at this time of the day, and there was no end of whispers about what Reuben Bennet was doing in the Butcher's Arms with the daughter of the local wise woman, Mrs. James. Mrs. James was a well-known figure in Totbrook as a finder of lost objects, fortune teller, and healer.

"I saw an image of a skull, in the middle of the teacup." Mary looked at me, expecting me to understand her.

"I take that to be a bad omen, but what has the position of the shape got to do with it?" I asked.

"Well the position of the omen means it refers to events about a week into the future, and with her inquiry relating to you, I took the omen to portend your death." Mary looked past me curiously.

"But what harm can Eleanour do to me? What part has she in my future?" I asked.

"Your cousin is behind you." She looked past me. At first I thought it symbolic, but as she persisted I turned to see that Eleanour was entering the pub alongside the newly promoted Joseph who was wearing a new star on each of his epaulettes.

"Station Inspector Rathbone, are you and my cousin in the habit of meeting without me now?" Joseph's pallid complexion began to turn as red as his sideburns and moustache.

"Where the bloody hell have you been? Your cousin and

122

I have been traipsing around for hours. All we got was some guff, begging your pardon ladies, about you exorcising a demon in St. Peter's church crypt." He pulled out a seat for Eleanour and began unbuttoning his coat. "Explain yourself!" He sat down opposite me and gave me a fixed stare.

"It was a load of superstitious nonsense; the Father believed Mary here to be possessed by the Devil," I said dismissively, to the disappointment of my cousin and the annoyance of Miss James.

We stayed a while in the pub. Mary and Eleanour became quickly enraptured of each other, discussing their shared interest in the paranormal at great length. Joseph, however, was much more reserved. He sat nursing his pint and occasionally making accusatory glances in my direction.

"Mary and I wish to be excused." Eleanour gestured towards the W.C. before they both scurried hastily away. Joseph fixed me with a stare.

"Well then, care to tell me what really went on, as opposed to the cock-and-bull story you told me two pints ago?" Ever since Joseph gained his recent promotion he had been getting better at detecting falsehood. He went for a swig of his beer.

"Mary was somewhat possessed. But not by a devil, she says. It was by a spirit guide called 'Tom Salt,' apparently." Joseph dribbled his beer momentarily.

"I would call that a load of old fanny if it weren't for what happened on the moor," he said as he wiped his moustache.

"He told me that I was going to die and that Eleanour would, inadvertently, play a role in it somehow." He looked at me sceptically.

"But how?" he asked dismissively.

"That is the problem. I have no idea," I replied.

"We best be careful then. I shall remain tight-lipped, don't you worry." He took another swig of his beer. The girls returned from the water closet.

Several days later, Eleanour had somehow managed to find me, even on a market day with the streets filled with Totbrook residents.

"I would never willfully cause you any harm, cousin," Eleanour said emphatically. Joseph had much to answer for.

"Joseph was not supposed to alarm you with it. I fancy it to be nonsense anyway," I said in an obvious attempt at deception. The lie was about as unconvincing as the sign reading, "All our fruit and vegetables are fresh from source" that Mr. Peebles was hanging in his window.

"I know you believe it to be true cousin. Besides which, you have spent the last week avoiding me and spending most of your free time in St. Peter's Church," she replied.

"Father Smethwick has been tutoring me on the subject of demonology. I have also been taking a few of my own precautions." I produced a pendant of a silver cross, which I had purchased from Mr. Hattersley's Jewellers, from inside my frock coat.

"Do you mean to ward me away cousin?" she quipped, her cheeks brightening.

"Besides which, I do not think that you can be saved by Father Smethwick's papish rituals; he will fall foul of the public worship act one of these days. Let us walk together for a while." She held out her hand.

We continued walking towards the Butcher's Arms. Joseph was waiting for us, and he was overdue for a rebuke. It was already dark as we approached Brook Street, where the Butcher's Arms was located, when a black two-horse carriage came careening out of the night towards us. The coachman was wearing his hat low and his collar high but his glaring eyes, which, though they were barely visible, betrayed his maniacal intent.

"Cousin!" I shouted, as I shoved Eleanour out of the way with all the force I could muster. The carriage bounded past us as the coachman cursed loudly in disappointment. Eleanour was lying directly underneath me and shaking with fright.

"Bastard!" I shouted, drawing my revolver ready to shoot at the thin sliver of the coachman's hat visible from behind the carriage as it was gradually shrinking into the distance.

"No! Cousin," Eleanour grabbed my arm, "he is fleeing!"

Rage was filling me, but she was correct. I could not shoot a man in the back.

"You are right, apologies for shoving you, cousin." I hastily replaced my revolver inside the jacket-holster I had fashioned for myself.

"Don't be absurd. You saved my life." Eleanour dusted her dress.

"I wasn't even going to the Butcher's Arms, it is a good thing you met." The realisation hit me at once that I would not have been here if I hadn't been walking with her.

"I think it is best we part company for the time being, cousin. Joseph will walk you home. Goodnight." I walked home at a furious pace, frequently glancing over my shoulder fearing the coachman's return. I slept barely a wink the entire night.

"Yes, Father, it appears 'Tom Salt' was right. I mean, I did almost die owing, however unwittingly, to my cousin." The priest smiled kindly. I had spent the last few mornings visiting the Vicar at St. Peter's after he had given his morning service.

"Yes, my boy, it was a good thing I sent for you. I called upon Miss James only yesterday to ask her about her well-being after that nasty business in the crypt." The vicar gave me a grave look.

"What did she say, Father?" I had spent the last few days purposefully avoiding Mary James, not out of fear of 'Tom Salt,' but due to her being accompanied seemingly everywhere by my cousin Eleanour.

"That is the thing, she cursed at me repeatedly and bid me to leave in no uncertain terms. Evidently that creature still has some kind of hold upon her." The priest smiled sadly.

"Would you like tea, Reverend Smethwick? Mr. Bennet?" Grant Fox, a well-built young man in his thirties brought over a tray of steaming hot tea mugs.

"If you wouldn't mind, deacon. Oh, and Mr. Bennet takes half a sugar and the tiniest pinch of milk." The priest dropped two cubes of sugar into his tea and a lot of milk. I took my mug from the tray and began stirring.

"The reason I asked you here Mr. Bennet was not just to drink tea, or to discuss Mary James and errant coachmen." He took a sip of his still steaming hot tea.

"No, Mr. Bennet. I brought you here to invite you to a select meeting of my most curious and learned parishioners." The priest handed me a small card;

The Society of Learned Seekers.
St. Peter's Church, Totbrook.
Chair: Father Reginald Smethwick.
Friday Evenings, Eight P.M. prompt.

126

"We meet every Friday night to discuss certain topics that are not suitable for my normal Sunday service." The priest sat back in his chair and smiled. I looked at the card. It was made of heavy paper and felt substantial in my hand.

"What do you discuss?" I took a sip from my tea. It was much too hot still. I feared I had burned my tongue.

"Much the same as we have been discussing the last few days. The supernatural, spirits, demons, and other such things. You will come, won't you?" He put his tea mug down and gave me an anticipatory look.

"Of course, Father." I had never been invited to join an exclusive club before. The vicar smiled and offered me a biscuit.

It was just before noon when I left the vicarage in search of some lunch when I was accosted by yet another close friend.

"I knew you would be here, Reuben." Joseph was leaning on a gatepost and wearing his uniform.

"Hello, Inspector Rathbone, my cousin isn't here is she? I'd rather not be killed by a mad coachmen today," I said acrimoniously.

"She had nothing to do with that, and you know it. There's no need to blame her." He shot me an angry look.

"I am sorry for being so harsh, but I do believe that 'Tom Salt' spoke the truth. The incident last night only convinced me more fully than before. I think it is best if I avoid her for the time being, and where she goes you tend to follow," I replied. Joseph was angered by the last observation as was evident by the deep frown on his face.

"I am not some kind of lovesick hound, and leastwise she isn't here at the moment, and I wondered if you fancied a pint in the Butcher's." He smiled almost as if by great effort, "Not seen any of you this past week, and Gregory is serving your favourite corned beef sandwiches."

"Give it up man! Why do you really want me to accompany you to the pub?" He swore under his breath before sighing in resignation.

"It wasn't my idea," He furtively looked about the vicarage yard and walked nearer. "It's Eleanour. She says Miss James wishes to speak with you at the Butcher's. It's urgent. I promised to deliver you there." He hung expectantly on the last word and fixed me with a pleading look.

"Two invitations in a day." I muttered. I followed Inspector Rathbone to the Butcher's Arms.

Of course she was there. Resplendent in what seemed to be a new dark blue bustle dress and sat in eager anticipation. By the side of her new best friend, Mary James, sat my cousin Eleanour Townley. I turned for the door.

"No! Wait, Reuben. Stay another moment more, please!" Her soft voice massaged my inflamed temper a fair deal.

"Cousin, I hold no grudge against you, but I really must avoid you for the time being," I protested.

"No, you don't." Mary James looked up from her half pint of Haddock's Ale. Her face was pale and of an urgent mien.

I walked cautiously over to the table and checked the chair before sitting down.

"It was not 'Tom Salt' you talked to in the crypt." Mary spoke very deliberately and with all seriousness.

"Then, who…"

"I will tell you what I know." She took a deep breath and began.

"About the day we met, I recollect little of what happened previously to you reviving me and bringing me here." Joseph

128

sat down on the chair next to me.

"I believe I was kidnapped by men from St. Peter's church. I am not sure, but I believe that Father Smethwick himself cast the spell that caused me to become possessed by whoever or whatever that creature was." She was struggling to remember something, but she did not reveal it to me.

"I find that hardly likely. Father Smethwick is a pious and devout Christian man," I replied, angry at the insinuation of heresy.

"Don't be a fool, cousin; they must have designs upon you for some reason or another. That is why Father Smethwick keeps inviting you over. Has he mentioned anything to do with a secret society of any kind?" Eleanour was flustered, she had clearly been taken in by Mary James' story.

"What is it, cousin?" Eleanour must have spotted me thinking, as she sometimes did.

"There was one thing..." I placed the card on the table.

"The Society of Learned Seekers?" Mary grasped the card and stared intently upon it. Mary James looked at the card with an apparent terror.

"I have heard that name before. I remember now, the priest officiating the ritual spoke that name." She threw the card down.

"It is just a society for men who are interested in the supernatural. Leastwise, why would Father Smethwick kidnap a woman to have her possessed by a demon?" I retrieved the card.

"He is fond of ritual, and here is the interesting part: the 'Saint Amy' he constantly refers to in his sermons, there is no such saint!" Eleanour produced a large tome from her seat and began flicking through it with the practised hand of a librarian's daughter.

"See: St. Amunia, St. Anacharius, but no Amy." I looked at the proffered page. She was correct. The priest often spoke of a "Saint Amy," a bringer of knowledge and guide to the ambitious.

"Then who is Saint Amy?" I asked, I had heard of folk saints but I suspected that my worst fear was playing out before my eyes.

"The Lesser Key of Solomon," Mary James muttered, almost to herself.

"What is the...?" I was interrupted.

"A grimoire of demonology. Amy is a fallen angel who promises his followers learning and influence," Eleanour replied.

"His?" I always assumed the saint was a woman.

"We best get 'round there then." Joseph supped the remainder of his pint up.

"No. Reuben must go to the meeting. We must catch the *Vicar in flagrante delicto*," Eleanour insisted. I made a start on the pint I had just ignored for a quarter of an hour.

We arranged not to be seen in public together the next day. Not until this whole thing was resolved. As I walked around the churchyard, I thought of all Father Smethwick had told me in the last few days and how the key to being safe from dark forces was to understand them.

The vicar had unorthodox views far outside of the mainstream of Anglicanism, that much was obvious to all of his parishioners, but his interest in demonology, which at first struck me as an eccentricity, may likely be something much more sinister.

Could he really be a heretic?

The demon I spoke to in the crypt – was it the "Saint Amy" that Father Smethwick frequently mentioned in his sermons?

What possible reason can Father Smethwick have for wanting me, Reuben Bennet, to join his society?

These questions echoed in my mind for much of the day. Having little else to do until I attended the meeting of "The Society of Learned Seekers," I found myself wandering the streets of Totbrook for most of the day, just to fill time.

I was walking down Holbarth Road, one of the main thoroughfares in and out of the town, when I spotted Mary James and Grant Fox, the deacon from St. Peter's Church, huddled in an alleyway between two houses. Grant's imposing figure towered over the diminutive but sturdy frame of Mary James. I took cover behind a garden wall on the other side of the road and observed. At first what I took for a conspiratorial meeting or canoodling, appeared as otherwise. Deacon Fox appeared to be bearing over a frightened Mary James who was cowering underneath the stern man's intimidation.

The situation intrigued me, and I wanted to see it play out, but more immediately I thought of the potential danger to Mary from the burly and aggressive man. He was unarmed so I fought the temptation to draw my revolver. Even being close friends with the local station inspector would not spare me from a murder charge this time. Just as I prepared myself mentally to break cover and charge the rogue, he ceased in his belligerence and began to walk away. I ducked deeper behind the wall and out of sight as he made his way past me and deeper into the town.

I broke cover as soon as the deacon was out of view and made for the alleyway. The gap between the houses was narrow, something commonly referred to as a "ginnel" hereabouts. I followed the first ginnel to its conclusion, but Mary James was nowhere to be seen. In this maze of alleyways and ginnels it would be a fool's errand to persist, so I made my way back home.

It was already getting dark by the time I made my way back to my lodging rooms. I had taken a rather circumlocutory route home owing to my reluctance to see the anticipated outcome of the night play out before me. After all, there is a difference between accepting something in your mind and accepting something in your heart, and I was unwilling to see the truth played out before my eyes.

I knew that what Eleanour and Mary had said made some sense, and after seeing Grant Fox intimidate Mary, it destroyed any lingering doubt I had in my mind as to what the truth of the matter was.

I donned my evening clothes – the ones I kept for the best moments. My finest white shirt, with its collar starched, sat underneath my black waistcoat and my violet colored cravat. My black trousers had been pressed at Mrs. Mulberry's laundry earlier in the day, and I had just polished my shoes two nights ago. I donned my black top hat with the low crown I wore to functions. I checked that my revolver still sat in my jacket-holster.

I moved quickly. My pocket watch told the time as being five minutes to eight. I knew it would take longer than five minutes at walking pace, so I ran through the streets in an effort to still be vaguely on time. Even so, I arrived at the Vicarage several minutes late and I could already hear Father Smethwick's voice as I reached the garden gate.

I inspected the whistle hanging from a string around my neck; Joseph had given me it the night before to use as and when required by circumstance. He had told me he would be in earshot. He was not wrong, for I could see the top of his helmet sticking out from the side of the house. I knew that the newly promoted Sergeant Black would be with him. I proceeded towards the doorway and rapped on the door;

Knock! Knock!

The lion-faced knocker on the large black door reverberated loudly in the stillness of the night.

"Mr. Bennet, so glad that you could join us. You had me worried you would not be in attendance." The priest smiled kindly.

"Forgive my lateness, Father. I had lost all track of time and had to hasten here as soon as I realized how late it was," I said almost as if all at once.

He laughed momentarily, "Do not worry for a moment about it, Mr. Bennet. Do come in. May I take your coat and hat?"

"Yes please, Father," I replied.

He took my coat and hat and escorted me into the sitting room where a half dozen men sat around in casual discussion.

Grant Fox sat beside a vacant armchair at the far end of the room. Edgar Townley, my uncle-by-marriage and town librarian, was seated next to him. Mr. Walsh, another deacon from St. Peter's, sat on the far end from them both, and Albert Twamley, a bank clerk at Stephenson's Bank on the high street, was seated next to him. I learned through introduction that the remaining two men, seated beside the vacant chair, were Mr. Graham, a wholesaler, and Mr. Taylor, a bootmaker.

"So Gentlemen, let us begin our meeting." The vicar smiled, his eyes appearing beady behind his freshly donned spectacles.

"Mr. Fox, show Mr. Bennet a copy of our club charter, if

133

you please." The vicar gestured to the deacon, who handed me a single sheet of paper. It was headed with a preamble:

The Society of Learned Seekers

For Seekers of the truth behind creation and greater understanding of the wider universe.

The rest of the document was a prosaic list of procedures and rules. As far as I could tell, it all looked very ordinary.

"Have you read it? Good, then let's proceed. Albert here was telling us about a ghost his daughter claimed to have seen in the still of night." The priest handed over to Albert Twamley, who continued his tale.

We listened to Albert's story of what his daughter Beatrice had seen. It was an intriguing story, one that had us all on the edge of our seats, but what shocked me was not the talk of apparitions hovering above Little Beatrice's bed or of objects moving of their own accord; it was the absolute lack of any resemblance to the meeting I had expected.

Where was the talk of black masses and demons?

Where were the robes and chants?

The incense and the blasphemous iconography?

I appeared to have been invited to a ghost club.

"Mr. Bennet, you look as if you are deep in thought. Do you care to add something to our discussion at all?" Deacon Walsh's voice broke me from my reverie.

"Sorry, I was just absorbed thinking of my own recent encounter," I said, thinking fast.

"Indeed, dear nephew. But which one?" My Uncle Edgar

said with a wry smile and the delight of the room.

"Well, I will start with the crypt incident. Perhaps there will be time later for tales of my other escapades. I was led to the church by Father Smethwick…" I regaled them with the story of the day to the rapt attention of the entire room, who gasped and pressed for more at the appropriate times. All except for Grant Fox, who sat staring at me as if watching for an error or falsehood.

"…and then I took the young lady to recuperate in the Butcher's Arms, where she was most shocked to hear the story I have just told you all." I faced a room full of delighted and intrigued faces brimming with questions.

"And have you faced any danger in line with Tom Salt's warning?" Grant Fox gave me a heavy stare, evidently knowing the answer. He had been present when I had told the vicar of the coachman after all.

"Yes, I believe you have, have you not Reuben? Something about a coach?" Father Smethwick pitched the question rather casually.

"Yes, I was almost hit by an errant coach-driver whilst in my cousin's company, a few nights ago. It absolutely convinced me of the demon's veracity." I addressed the answer to a curious Grant Fox, as I was starting to realise the conspiracy that had been playing out around me.

"So you would say that there truly was a demon possessing Miss James?" Grant Fox asked, the sighting of him earlier in the day had revealed the truth of the matter to me and I knew what he expected me to say.

"Like I said, I was absolutely convinced of it, Deacon Fox, that is until I saw you threatening Miss James in a ginnel just off Holbarth Road earlier today." Grant Fox's face began to turn to anger. The deacon was infuriated. "What was it you were saying to her to make her so afraid?" The rest of the room looked to the deacon and implored him to give an explanation.

"Well Mr. Fox, is this true? What have you got to say for yourself?" Father Smethwick turned to him, barely suppressing the shock and anger at the deacon.

"You know full bloody well, Father." Grant Fox swore, he stood up and pointed at Father Smethwick.

"He made me do it. He made me warn her off. She was getting too close to the truth!" Grant Fox spoke passionately, keen to be seen as relieving himself from a great burden he had carried unwillingly for so long.

"Father Smethwick has been in cahoots with the 'Tom Salt' Mr. Bennet here spoke of. Except his name is not 'Tom Salt' at all, and his true identity is 'Amy,' a fallen angel and demonic entity!" Grant Fox let the accusation hang in the air as the room filled with outrage and disbelief at the wild claim.

"Well, what do you say then, Father Smethwick?" Mr. Townley posed inquisitively. The elderly priest was evidently upset at the charges laid upon him by his subordinate and struggled to answer;

"I-I took you under my wing Mr. Fox. How-how dare you accuse me of such blasphemy!?" The priest looked upon his protégé in evident disbelief.

"I have proof! Gentlemen, we must go to the church where evidence of dark communion abounds!" Grant Fox pointed to the door, and with that much busying was made as the assembled men left their seats in search of their coats and hats.

Father Smethwick was in terrible shock, struggling to get out of his chair as he shook with the stress of the situation.

"Father, do you require my assistance?"

"Yes, my boy, if you would be so kind?" He looked at me wide eyed and in fear of what would be revealed in the crypt.

"Father, I think I understand what is happening. I believe Deacon Fox concocted this whole thing with Mary James' help." The vicar looked at me curiously. I helped him out of his chair and towards the door.

The rest of the society were already leaving through the garden gate when we closed the door behind us. I looked towards Joseph, peering out from the side of the far wall he had sequestered himself behind and gave him the signal to follow behind us. Father Smethwick was about to speak when I put a finger to my lips and whispered, "All will become clear in time, Father."

We followed the rest of the society to the church where Grant Fox asked Deacon Walsh for the key, a large old fashioned device and opened up the great doors.

The deacons lit candles and ushered the society towards the crypt amid great whispers and excitement. With the attention of the group fixed solely on the matter at hand, I signalled for Inspector Rathbone and Sergeant Black, an awkward and gangly man, to follow us through the open church doors.

"Wait here. I will whistle," I mouthed to Joseph after the huddled mass had made its way into the room adjoining the sanctuary.

I helped Father Smethwick down the stairs towards the crypt. The society all stood in frozen horror at the crude altar that sat underneath an upturned cross at the head of the room. It was the place Mary James had been sitting when I last entered. A dead chicken lay upon it, accompanied by a large old

137

grimoire bound in leather. I was shocked by the lengths that Deacon Fox had descended in order to sew his deceit.

"Father Smethwick is in league with the devil!" Grant Fox loudly proclaimed to the excitement of the crowd.

"No! No! It is not true!" Father Smethwick pleaded to the already decided company.

"Well, what are you waiting for, Mr. Bennet? This man has proven his infernal allegiance with his attempt upon your life, has he not? You are friends with the new station inspector, have this apostate vicar arrested!" The assembled crowd shouted in agreement and jostled the terrified old man.

"Unhand me! He speaks lies!" Father Smethwick shouted in vain as two members of the crowd arrested his attempt at flight. I swallowed a lump in my throat for seeing the priest so poorly treated and turned to ascend the first few steps and blew my whistle twice.

"Right, what do we have here then!" Joseph and Sergeant Black came running down the stairs.

"Arrest this man, sergeant. He is in league with the devil." The two policemen were horrified and disgusted by the sight of the altar, and made to arrest Father Smethwick.

I stopped them both just as the sergeant had readied his handcuffs.

"Inspector, gentlemen. The truth of the matter has yet to be revealed!" I shouted loudly, Grant Fox looked incredulous at my interruption.

"Deacon Fox is behind this whole charade. I would have been taken in by all of this were it not for his stage school theatrics. He placed these items here and encouraged the vicar to invite me here so as to act as his witness." The room became alive with whispers and confusion.

"Grant Fox attended the same stage school as our mutual friend, Mary James. Didn't you Mr. Fox?"

"Yes I did. What of it?" He said sheepishly, evidently flustered by the revelation.

"This whole affair has been a ploy, most likely to allow Deacon Fox to take control of the church upon his upcoming ordination as a priest. He had Mary James convince me of the reality of the demon. Most likely he was also the one who attempted to run me down with a coach a few nights ago!"

Grant Fox was trembling with fury and confusion as the assembled company looked at him with grave disappointment and anger.

"He has stitched me up; he must be in league with the old man!" Grant began frantically looking for an escape.

"You may try and convince our company of your lies Mr. Fox, but I do know you to have been previously employed as a coach driver before you came to me so impressed by this church and its building. Were you not also the one who told me all about this 'Saint Amy?' I cannot believe you could conspire against me and the Lord God so wickedly!" Father Smethwick exclaimed, having broken free from his now loosened restraint.

"You pompous, old lying bastard!" Grant Fox burst towards the priest in a rage before being grabbed and secured by the crowd. Sergeant Black and Joseph moved to arrest him as he struggled against his restraint, cursing all present.

Everybody followed the arresting officers and Grant Fox upstairs. Everybody except the old priest, who stopped me just before I followed them out of the crypt.

"Thank you, my boy. I knew he was envious of my position, but I had no idea to what depths he would plumb to unseat me. You have done me a very good turn." He smiled and shook my hand firmly before accompanying me up the stairs.

Grant Fox died mysteriously in his cell several days later while awaiting trial. The town had been told it was suicide, but I had viewed the body not long after and was left with an unsettling feeling. He had died of asphyxiation; lacerations were clearly visible around his neck.

The town greeted the news of the loss of such an evil man with great joy as you might expect, but I suspected that he had not died of his own hands.

A few days later I interrogated Mary James in the Butcher's Arms on why she had been party to the deacon's theatrics.

"I was not lying to you." She protested, angry at my accusation. "I was possessed by the demon. Grant Fox was telling the truth about Father Smethwick. He performed the rites that led to my possession!"

"But why then did Grant Fox threaten you in the ginnel?" I was in disbelief. She was persistent even after Deacon Fox's death.

"He wanted my help to stop Smethwick, but I was too afraid to return to the church. Amy made an attempt upon my soul, and only Tom Salt's intervention saved me. I didn't want to risk it again. The demon has designs upon this town. The threat upon your life is real, Mr. Bennet."

She was not lying. I would meet "Saint Amy" again.

The Bizarchives

Lex and the Horror of Bernwick Hollows
by Dave Martel

The town of Bernwick. A sultry valley borough nestled betwixt the rolling bosoms of the Valelands. A commonly traversed resting place for weary travelers who prefer trekking the midlands instead of faring the treacherous waters of the black coast. Although its natives are quite hospitable, Bernwick is no stranger to its share of scandal. While most who frequent the unmarked roads of Grimeorth are purveyors of merchantry, the lawless wanders and wilds attract derelicts of subhuman instinct. The deranged and deviant oft slither their way into quaint communities such as Bernwick to quench their vile thirsts, only to slink back into the desolate mists to live among the unholy wraiths and hungering monstrosities that lurk throughout this cursed realm.

Lex halts his steed just before the town gate as the baking evening sun descends behind the stabbing ebon peaks of the distant trollspine mountains. He dismounts behind a small two-wheeled cart as its driver passes by a single guarding spearman in a studded leather hauberk. Lex approaches with reins in hand. After a quick investigative glance from the guard, he nods to signal him through. Like most settlements that dot these lands, Bernwick appears tediously ordinary. A main cobblestone street splits through its entirety with various stands, storefronts, and inns lined along it. Behind them clusters of erratically placed residential cottages of humble construction. Earthen plaster and stone with thatched roofs and bellowing chimneys casting grey puffs into the lingering smog above.

As the humid evening wanes, a cool night breeze ushers out the wafting aromas from the kitchens and cookeries as the shopkeepers and standing merchants lock up for the evening. Every corner and tavern stoop is populated by small gaggles of patrons and locals mingling with pints in hand. The choiring chatter and conversations occasionally interrupted by a boisterous outburst of some drunken chucklehead with his boots propped up. The stern-faced Lex cracks a smile, entertained by the carefree jubilance of inebriated yokels. Among the colorful chorus of unwinding townsfolk, Lex hears the faint sobs of a nearby woman. He turns his head to see the cart that passed through before him at the gates, parked behind a nearby building. He approaches to see its driver, a young woman wrapped in a pale blue hooded cloak still perched on the front-facing bench. Leaned forward near collapsing in defeat, with her face buried in her palms. Her whispered cries indiscernible, muffled by her tear-soaked sleeves.

"What misfortune bewitches you, m'lady?" Lex inquires with baritone conviction.

Startled, the girl abruptly sits straight, quickly wiping her face with her sleeve. She replies with a poorly composed tone avoiding eye contact. "Good sir, I am in no need of wares or service. I am simply having a moment of grief. Now please, be on your way."

144

"I am no seller of wares, young one. I am called Ser Lucious Lex. I am a slayer of fiends, and I offer my aid at no cost. If my skills may be of help to you, ask one of the inn-keepers. I doubt my presence will go unnoticed." He pats the edge of the cart's driver bench and turns to leave.

"Wait."

Lex turns back to face the woman as she halts his departure.

"Follow me to my family's inn. We've been closed for a few weeks but still have soft beds and provisions enough for a hot meal."

Ser Lucious nods and gestures for the woman to lead forth. The cart moves slowly as it bumps and creaks on the uneven cobblestone road. At the end of the main way, tucked back a few paces sits a terrifically crafted two-story stone-work building. On one side a storehouse, the other an empty stable. Hanging above the center sitting doorway of the inn swings an ornate rectangular sign that reads "Talbert's Bread and Brew." The girl climbs down from her cart and trots up to the main door to unlock it with a keyring concealed under her cloak. She approaches Lex's horse and grabs the reins from his hand.

"I unlocked the door for you, Ser Lex. Please go upstairs and find a room to your liking. After you bathe and dress I should have supper prepared for you. Please go, I'll stable your horse for you," she urges.

Lex bobbles his head in brief contemplation before releasing his stead into the maiden's care. Upon entry, Lex scans the dimly lit, empty establishment. Although modest, the tavern is impeccably furnished with cushioned stools, polished oak bar tops and a masterful stone hearth with a large antlered beast mounted above it. On the far side, a set of carpeted steps with smooth wooden rails lead up a staircase partially illuminated by dying lantern sconces. With a more than usual labored gaunt, Lex makes his way towards the bar and leans over. From behind he pulls out a brown decanter filled with some unnamed spirit. With a pop of the cork he tips the swill back and takes a deep chug. With a grunt and a strained gulp he grips the rails and struggles up the steps.

Lucious doffs his battered plate and faded cuirass placing them in a locker on top of his mail and gambeson. After closing the box he hears a rap at the door. Lex turns the knob and pulls it ajar.

"Hot water for your basin, Ser Lex. I'll leave it here in the hallway. There's a hot stew on the stove and fresh bread in the oven. Come down when you're ready." The woman skirts off.

Lex fills his basin with the water and gives himself a warm wash. The heat soothes the countless scars and many physical malformations all over his brutish physique. He stands two heads taller than the average man with a thick, bearish visage. But every move is nagged by a constant ache from his body being hopelessly broken, healed, and broken again. The only remedy for his constant pain being a frequent warm bath and stiff drink. His gift of healing magic comes at a price. Torn flesh, mangled innards and shattered bones unnaturally reassembled and reformed over and over becoming more gnarled and twisted with each healing. Few men, if any, could suffer such a tormented existence. But what drives this man is not of this world. His soul was shaped upon an anvil of wrath and tempered in hateful hellfire burning with the calamitous rage of a thousand suns. Last of the last of the Tivarian Order. When men have nightmares, they see devils. When devils have nightmares, they see Lucious Lex.

An enchanting scent permeates into Lex's room as he finishes fastening his shirt and trousers. The hearty aroma of seasoned meat and hot yeast trigger a roiling rumble in his neglected stomach. As if he's being summoned by a siren's song, the freshened warrior descends down the stairs into the empty dining area. On a roundtop table in the middle of the lit room sits a perfectly laid out dinner placement. Empty copper bowl with utensils, cloth napkin, and pitcher with ale froth foaming over the side. Lex sits and tips the pitcher to pour the golden ale into a pewter pint. He lifts his eyes to see the young woman come scampering in from a back room lugging a steaming iron pot. Lex pauses stricken by the form of the maiden he hadn't noticed before. Youthful and rosy, her curly strawberry hair pulled back into tail. Earthy hazel eyes partially covered by curled bangs. Milky fair freckled skin and full pink lips upon her round face. A light flowing linen dress poorly concealing her voluptuous curves.

"My grandmother's recipe, Ser Lex. I pray that you enjoy" the girl scoops a wooden ladle into the creamy brown stew and fills her guest's bowl nearly to the brim. Lex fixates on her beautiful shifting physique as she scampers to the counter to bring over a metal plate with hot bread sliced and fanned out for proper display.

"All this is quite unnecessary, m'lady."

"Alora. Call me Alora. It is I who should be addressing you with titles," she assures as she sits down across from him.

"So, you've heard of me?" Lex asks with attention focused on blowing the steam from his spoonful of hot stew.

"Of course. Who hasn't heard the tales and rumors of Lucious Lex the slayer?" She waves her hands sarcastically.

"What of the rumors?" Lex halfway inquires with a

mouthful of bread.

"That you were born of beast and your presence is known by the stench of death"

"And what is your impression of the beastman before you, Alora?" Lex smirks.

"Although you are much larger than I could have imagined, you seem human enough to me. But the second part is true. Hence why I offered you a wash." Alora raises her brows with a smile. The two share a friendly chuckle.

"So, tell me Alora. How may I repay this wonderful hospitality?" Lex leans back as Alora fills his bowl and ale a second time.

"It's my brother and mother. They're missing. Since my older sister passed my mother has developed an obsession with brewing medicinal concoctions for any possible future sickness that my brother and I may catch. For this most recent salve she needed corvus root, a plant that only grows in caves. Less than a week ago she left to go find it. After she didn't come back, my brother left to go search for her. He hasn't come back either," she explains

"What about your father?" Lex inquires taking the last bites of bread.

"My father died before I was born. He fought in the last mongrel crusade. Both he and my grandfather were legion and fell during the massacre. They were named Talbert. The namesake of this tavern." Alora assumes a solemn frown.

"Heroes. My father fell then, too. I wear his armor. I'm the last of the Tivarian Order, the fraternity your family hails from as well. Your brother inherits this lineage," Lex says profoundly.

"My brother has a different father. My mother married

the local baker. A drunk fool but left us with some wonderful recipes before he ran off with some harlot," she snarls.

"So what is this cave?" Lex asks.

"Bernwick Hollows. The locals say it's a portal to the demonic realms of Murkwood, and those who go in are dragged into the underworld by fiends. My mother said these were fool's tales from illiterate drunks and those who didn't return fell down into dark crevices. Either way, I just want my family to come home." Alora chokes as a few tears trickle down her rosy cheeks.

Lex wipes his face with the cloth napkin and stands up. "Draw me a map to the caverns, and place it here on the table. I will head there at first daylight." Lex takes his leave as Alora begins gathering the dishes. He climbs the steps back to his room for the night.

Before the morning sun crests Lex comes down the stairs donned in full armor. A fairly well drawn map sits on the cleaned table where he had eaten the night before. After a thorough examination he folds the map and sticks it into a belt pouch. In chilling morning air he unhooks his horse and rides off through the town at full gallop and down into the valley. Alora's map proved true. A few hours' ride and another hour's hike through the sparse pine forest lead Lex to the large dark cave mouth of Bernwick Hollows. After tying his stead to a nearby tree he descends within the damp cavern. With each step further into the subterranean hole the outer light becomes more faint, obscuring Lex's vision. Condensation cascading from jagged stalagmite tips drip into lonely puddles, casting ghostly echoes in the near distance. Every step becomes more treacherous upon the slimy rock and rubble beneath his feet as he trudges deeper into pitch black darkness.

With a whispered hymn he holds up his spiked mace,

and it brightens with a heavenly iridescent glow. The trusty bludgeon illuminates his immediate vicinity to reveal much of the same chaotic cave features. Lex follows the corridor as it bends and winds down deeper into the hazy depths. Every so often he is startled by the echoes of scuttering taps from crawling legs. He waves his magic torch about scanning for predatory subsurface denizens, but the cave's reverberation makes locating near impossible. Every slithering shadow when illuminated reveals to be nothing. Lex takes a step down through a ridged threshold to see a bit of shining sunlight emblazing something astounding. He lurches closer, offhand maintaining balance on the coarse cave walls and steps into the light.

The near sounding of casual speech reaches his ears. Before him a large cavernous chamber brightened by sunlight. In the middle shimmers a serene pool of crystal water. As his eyes adjust, the chamber comes into full vision. A lavishly decorated alcove with stone walls and marble floors. Relaxing in the pool and wading about are beautiful women in scanty attire. All around, various furnishings and cushioned chairs where patrons enjoy decadent goblets of wine. Lex cautiously enters attempting to draw little attention. To his side a gathering of low sitting pillowed seats. Engrossed in them a few people casually dressed. He scoots to the chairs and leans down to a napping woman.

"Excuse me madam, I am searching for the owners of Talbert's Bread and Brew from Bernwick."

The woman continues to sleep undisturbed. Across from her the frail voice of a young man answers.

"My mother and I run Talbert's along with my sister Alora. Will she be here soon?" The dark haired boy replies. Upon further inspection the boy appears emaciated with sunken eyes.

"I am here on behalf of your sister, Alora. She asked me to fetch you and your mother. Is she here?" Lex asks with unease.

An older ginger woman in plain dress raises shaky fingers "Yes dear, I will be home soon. Alora needn't worry. It's been ages since I've enjoyed the shoreside. Especially one as pristine as this'n."

The boy chimes in "We've worked so hard since my father left. It's such a relief to enjoy being out in nature like this. No drunken oafs shouting, no bar fights. Just the mountain breeze."

Lex gets a puzzled sneer, "shoreside? mountain breeze?"

He slowly lowers his belly to the floor and covers his nose and mouth with his cloak. His sight blurs and distorts as the pool of relaxing maidens transforms into a ghastly murky pond with bobbing and bloated corpses. His surroundings morph back into the jagged cavescape. Hallucinatory furnishings reveal their true horrific appearance. A slimy cavern floor littered with scattered bones and shredded human remains. The chairs around the chamber, thick stringent webbing with deflated carcasses of animals and humans. Several of them are mounted by hideous arachnid creatures sucking the liquified guts from their torsos through a syringe-like tongue appendage. Lex turns to Alora's beloved family to see they are stuck to large webs, cocooned in slimy adhesive regurgitant.

Leaping to his feet, Lex begins to hack at the webs around them, jostling and freeing them from their oozy cells. In a numbed daze, the two don't even react to the disturbance. All around the chamber the creatures scurry out of every tunnel and crevice alerting, one another with an abominable chattering choir of clicks and gurgles. As Lex frees the pair, the dog-sized creatures descend upon him. Thorax of a lanky legged spider with numerous wispy sensory apparatuses. Bulbous pulsing abdomen housing a curved stinger oozing with milky toxin. Sprouting from the front of their bodies a dwarfed humanoid torso with two freakish bony jointed arms and three-pronged claw hands. Their heads, perversely manlike but spherical. Randomly dotted with countless unblinking insectoid eyes all across the front of their skulls. When these mockeries of nature close in to attack, their grotesque jaws unhinge to reveal a maw full of hooked fangs. Nightmarish, straw-like tongue that telescopes out to half their body length.

Lex finally frees both of Alora's kin but senses the leaping monster attempting to strike from behind. With his boot to its abdomen, Lex drives the creature to the stone, pinning its pulsing stinger. It snaps viciously and lunges its daggered tongue into the hero's chestplate only to ricochet off. With his gauntleted grip he tears the tongue from the monster's mouth. With incredible reflex he avoids the desperate bites and grabs hold of the fiend's black-skinned head. With foot anchoring the body, Lex twists and ratchets the foul cranium, tearing it from the body. The beast twitches and curls as it sprays yellow bug guts. A second arachnoid pounces stinger-first but clangs into the immoveable shield now in the firm grip of Lex's offhand. With a crushing downward swing, the warrior's mace collides with the creature's head, bursting it into yellow mush. A third drops from the ceiling, but Lex firmly holds his shield overhead. When the devil collides, Lex thrusts the monster to the side falling directly into a cave spike, impaling itself.

The battle continues with Lex swinging, smashing, and obliterating an uncountable number of these sinister monstrosities. Yet the onslaught grows ever fervent as hordes of the crawling horrors pour out from every cave orifice. He loudly chants the illumination hymn and his yellow stained mace flashes with blinding brilliance. The insurmountable throng of despicable man-spiders shriek in pain as they recoil from the searing divine light. Thousands of little clicks from their crawling steps congest the chamber's soundspace as they frantically attempt to scurry into holes away from the light. Lex holds his mace proudly as a deterrent as he scoops up the pair and hoists them onto his shoulder, one stacked upon the other. With a bull's strength, Ser Lucious stomps up through the threshold and into the corridor. He slips and skates, losing footing with every fifth step. At quarter speed the slayer summons all his might to escape the cave, but the scuttering crowd begins to follow suit. A chase ensues.

From every portal and crack the creatures poke their heads out as Lex passes through, but as his shining mace fills his vicinity with illumination, they recoil back. Just out of the reach of the light, hundreds of them blanket every surface of the cave from top to bottom. One false step, and the three of them will be torn to pieces. A grotesque feast for these hellish abominations. One drops down before Lex and launches its knife tongue appendage. Lex side steps to shield the rescued victims but the bladed tongue bypasses his plate and deeply slashes the underside of his bicep. It immediately recoils in full blaze of the burning light. It tries to shield its eyes, but Lex delivers a devastating horizontal blow, breaking its hands and pulverizing its squishy face. In the distance, the soft glow of evening sun breaks through the darkness. Lex cuts loose a roar of determination as he trudges forth, each exhausted step closer to salvation.

Finally, the winded hero emerges into the sunlight. On his heels the spiders stop in their tracks, seething and hissing in anguish scurrying back into the shadows of the cave. Lex lumbers over to his horse and slumps the two cocooned victims over his horse and unhooks its reins. Upon his stead he trots by the cave entrance. From the darkness, thousands of tiny and glowing red eyes peer out at him. He triumphantly holds up his mace that is no longer glowing. The horde flinches at the sight of the mace and collectively screech in disapproval. Lex gallops off with a smug grin.

Nightfall descends upon Talbert's Bread and Brew when a pound at the door alerts Alora from her seat. She rushes to the door and flings it open to see her missing family members standing in the doorway and leaning on one another as they come to their senses. Alora explodes into joyous tears as wraps them both in an ecstatic hug. She helps them inside and sits them down. Immediately after, Alora comes charging out to Lex mounted upon his horse in the middle of the street.

"I knew you could do it! Whoever speaks ill of you, may they suffer in Murkwood! You are a blessing from heaven, Ser Lucious Lex. The Gods sent you to us." She sobs into his leg as he straddles his horse.

He reaches down and peels her off of his boot "The tales about the cave were true. There are friends there. Far too numerous to slay. Explorers get subdued by poison air, and the monsters feast on them. Tell the locals to stay far away."

She takes a step back with palms clasped "You're bleeding. Why don't you stay another night and let me patch you up? I'm sure you'll find that my bed is far more comfortable."

Lex cocks his head staring off down the road. "M'lady Alora, you are an enchantress. However, if I left you with child there would be no possibility of you wedding a good husband. A husband you need to care for your family and business. I will return again for that wonderful stew. If you are unmarried and still hold your beauty, I will happily bed you. Farewell, Alora"

154

Tears stream down her rosy cheeks as Lex gallops off into the night.

"Farewell to you, too, Ser Lex... my guardian angel."

Alora wipes her tears away and turns to go back inside. After finishing up the last of the reheated stew Alora helps her disoriented brother and mother to their beds. She tucks them both in, squeezes them tightly, and kisses them on their foreheads. After putting out their lights she makes her way downstairs to lock up the doors and gather the dishes. Startled, she drops the dishes on the floor. She listens in horror at the sound of scuttering taps on the rooftop. Hundreds of glowing little red eyes peer through the windows from the darkness.

To Play the Hero
by Emre Bilgin Tan
continued from "Atli's Folly" in The Bizarchives: Issue #1

The mewing of speckled gulls screened the air with noise. The regular rhythm of a series of oars plunging into water and rising again mixed with the creaking of the ship's hull. Berfrand watched the gulls flapping their wings far above the masts. They circled like dots over the far shores on both banks of River Gragus. At occasion, he sighted them plunging into sprawling oak woods, thickly grown on the hills beyond the distant banks, but those sights were too far away for the rest of the crew to watch with equal joy.

The sun was high above on the cloudless, blue sky, and though it scorched the earth about, the frequent breeze from the south-east kept the crew cool.

"—Well yes! I had spoken to Prince Dragan about our schedule, but he wanted to leave early," continued Captain Zelimir. He was a sturdy man, though of a smaller stature, and with a complexion darkened over the years with constant exposure to the sun.

"You reckon Lady Yasna vexed him endlessly for a return trip?" Berfrand drew his gaze from the endless sights about the ship. His eyes had a tendency to stray, which was seldom curbed.

"Oh I'm sure of it!" The captain spoke. "Lady Yasna has never liked those southern cities. I've served as a royal captain for the past fifteen years, and never once in those fifteen years has she requested to sail south. Not once! I'm sure a young woman like her is quickly bored there, what's with all the councils, and meetings, and so forth."

Berfrand nodded and raised an eyebrow as merchant Gellius budged into the conversation. He was a fat man, with a large, elaborate tunic and a cloak strewn over his generous figure. Though he was fair for a southerner--with a pink tint across his face---his features were still strange for Berfrand.

"Ah, what do we have here?" Gellius spoke as he rubbed his hands. A funny expression spread across his face. "Captain! Will you not introduce me to this young man?"

"Ah, surely, Gellius!" Zelimir startled. "This is— well! He's a trusted friend of our prince— around here he's named—"

Berfrand, seeing how the captain was about to blunder over his words, stepped in and introduced himself with a slight nod. "I'm Berfrand of the Northlands, an old friend of the royal family. May the stars bless our meeting, merchant-man."

"Oh, likewise, my dear friend!" Gellius exclaimed and gave a bow too respectful for Berfrand's status. "I would like to presume that friends of the royal family are also friends of mine, for my guild has long traded with the court."

"Unfortunate for that relationship to have come to an end, I suppose?" Berfrand asked.

The merchant's face dimmed and, for a brief moment,

Berfrand noticed his happy guise fall apart. Gellius was an expert at hiding his emotions, however, and he quickly renewed his smile.

"Ah, surely," he said, "it's a shame that King Kazimir has seen it fit to terminate our partnership. Business is business, however, and a productive enterprise is never endless, as my years of experience have taught me," Gellius wagged his finger as he leaned slightly forward as though he were speaking to a child. The gesture was mildly amusing to Berfrand, as he towered over Gellius almost by two heads. From that angle, the merchantman resembled a small, plump pig gloating about his profession.

"— as I've said," the merchant continued, "we can never be too sad that a profitable enterprise has reached an end. In this business, one grows accustomed to such changes. Besides, It wasn't *my* guild alone that suffered from the king's new legislation. All of the other southern merchants are now at a disadvantage."

"Indeed, Gellius," Berfrand added, "though I was surprised to see their representatives turn up for the meeting. Assuming you all knew of the king's intentions beforehand, I thought many would've been on the road looking for new patrons."

Berfrand's eyes trailed languidly over the three decks of the large galley. It was a royal ship, much longer and wider at the hull than any other vessel he had seen. There was a long main deck separating the fore and aft castles, and on this main deck were situated about twenty-five benches. There was a main walkway running amidship, with the benches set diagonally to it on either side. It had just occurred to Berfrand how crowded the ship's deck truly was. On each bench were three rowers, and several officers armed with bows and crossbows strolled on the walkways. If the rowers hadn't been sitting down and slouching forward, then the main deck would've been alive with dozens of bodies shuffling on the gangplanks.

"—oh we certainly would have. I myself have sent my agents to seek new contracts abroad. With new lords that might equal the great king in their generosity—"

"Like the Emperor himself?" Berfrand locked eyes with the merchant, and Gellius flinched in fear. Few men could manage to bear the gaze of an Elf-man.

"Well—I—surely that is an opportunity for us merchants. But I would—" Gellius blabbered.

"Of course, you would consult the Emperor!" Berfrand exclaimed. "Emperor Theakos and King Kazimir's ancestors have long vied for this Vale of Gragus. If one of the greatest rulers of the region rejects you, then you'll seek patronage from the other."

"Well, surely, but—" the merchant kept blabbering, and rubbing his hands in distress.

"Surely, Gellius, that's how politics work. I've contended with Theakos' delegates before, I know how their hunger looms over the southern cities. You, of course, being a southerner yourself, will find it more fitting to serve the man who your people once called their liege,"

Berfrand fixed his eyes on the merchant again. He was growing tired of city delegates, merchants, and guild-masters. For the last four months he had accompanied the royal princes as they had traveled from city to city, announcing new legislations, and conferring judgement on local matters. For the last four months he had born the endless noise and the bustle of overcrowded southern cities. When he had heard that Prince Dragan had resigned to sail back north early, he was the first man on board. In a way, Berfrand could understand Princess Yasna very well.

The merchant's eyes swiveled back and forth between Zelimir and Berfrand. The captain was carefully holding back a laughter. "Well, that is surely wrong my lord," Gellius tried to continue, "we southerners aren't necessarily—"

"Of course It was wrong," Berfrand interjected again, "my apologies. The Emperor is more than a man, of course. It would be a mistake to label him as a simple mortal. For you southerners, I reckon it would be accurate to name him a *hero*," Berfrand took care to lade his voice with condescent. "Regardless, Gellius, I'm rather tired of today's heat, and would like to draw to my quarters below deck. Good day!" Berfrand nodded, and without caring to look at the merchant, sauntered past the two men and made his way down the stairs of the stern deck.

"What a peculiar man!" Gellius exclaimed, gawking at tall man striding away.

Captain Zelimir grinned and put a hand on the merchant's shoulder. "I've served the royal family for the last fifteen years, Gellius, and let me tell you something. I've never once had a boring day with that man on deck," the captain laughed deeply from his belly, much to the grief of the fat merchant.

The Immortal Emperor, thought Berfrand. Some distant figure he was, almost mythic in the minds of the people, but very real for those who lived further south. Of course, he couldn't have been anything but some sort of an Elf, or an

Elf-man, like Berfrand himself. A vestige of the distant past, the member of a forgotten race. Those with elf blood were longer-lived than normal men. The more sinister possibilities with regards to the Emperor's nature Berfrand preferred to keep locked in the back of his mind.

King Kazimir's forefathers had fought against the legions of the same man, and for the last fifty or so years the River Gragus and its vale had been the stage for those conflicts. Yet, peace had been attained, a tenuous, ever-fragile balance between the two powers over the vale. But now, King Kazimir had seen it fit to terminate his contracts with the southern merchant guilds, and many of them had thus been summoned to the City of Ernedin. There, the eldest prince, together with the royal representatives, had announced the new terms for business.

Did war loom over them? King Kazimir had not divulged his intentions, but war seemed the most likely possibility. The southern merchants brought lucrative trade to Kazimir's realm, but in return they acted as spies for the Emperor. Everyone up north in Dvaziga were aware of it but had resigned to ignore it. Kazimir had deemed it a necessary cost for the wealth that flowed. That is, until recently. If the merchants like Gellius acted often as spies, it was prudent to cut ties with them before waging war. Did Kazimir really plan an invasion? If so, why hadn't he notified his own sons?

"The river is beautiful today," Dragan finally broke the silence. The two friends had been standing still on the edge of the fore deck for the last few minutes, watching the calm waters. Gragus was almost 10 furlongs wide, and its waters were a deep blue. Further away towards the banks the colour took a thin, greyish hue before terminating in brown, foundered banks of dirt. Even further beyond, the sight of Berfrand seized the shapes of undulating hills covered over with tall grasses and trees. Below, towards the banks were huddles of reeds, dancing in shades of yellowing green. The blue sky had turned pinkish red as the dusk sank deeper.

"Indeed, it is," Berfrand answered pensively after a long silence. "Like on that day when we had first met. How old were you then, five?" he asked without turning his head.

"Four. Your memory is sketchy," Dragan answered, smiling.

"I was seven, if I recall well. Your father's estate, near Stenport..." Berfrand's features tensed as he struggled to remember.

A wind blew from the south and waved the flag on the main mast. The banner bore the image of the Dvazigan eagle, double-headed, painted in white over a mantle of deep blue, and bearing a star under each wing.

"I remember well, though, how Mezamir had insisted on dueling me," Berfrand continued. "Your brother couldn't bear the fact that his father had welcomed a young boy into the family," he laughed. It was rare to see him smile, let alone laugh as freely as now. Dragan had noticed it, and his deep, blue eyes glazed over his friend's face. How rare was it, but how valuable due to it.

"Ah, my older brother was always a bit too proud. Even back then he loved playing the hero."

"Indeed, and your calmness was one thing he could rarely tolerate, especially when he required otherwise."

The sun had westered completely, and the last of its sinking lights were leaving the wide skies. At once, something disturbed the peace. Berfrand spotted shadows scuttling on the far bank. They were fast. With abrupt moves they rushed from hill to hill. It was hard to make out what they were, but with such speed he guessed they could only be horsemen.

"Something's moving on the other side," Berfrand spoke suddenly as he bristled up.

"I can't see anything. Are you sure—"

"I am," Berfrand cut off. "My eyes can see further than normal men, remember?"

Dragan swallowed audibly. Then, turning towards the main deck, he cried out for a man to rush over towards the stern and watch for movements on the far shore. The rowers had set their oars for the evening, so the main deck was lively with men walking about and chatting with one another, or otherwise digging into their evening rations. With the prince's order, confused heads swiveled about, looking for the shadowy figures. Whispers and shouts went wheeling in the crowd, and the passengers scattered about the decks waited in anticipation.

"Can't see anything, my lord!" called the seaman from the aft deck.

"What did you spot?" asked Zelimir attentively as he approached the wale.

"Shadows!" cried Berfrand across the deck. "They're moving fast. I reckon horsemen"

"Maybe they're wolves," said one of the archers on the main deck.

"Nay. They're too large," Berfrand quashed.

"Are you sure about this?" Dragan whispered, tugging at his friend's arm.

"I trust my sight, Dragan. It hasn't failed me ever," Berfrand turned his eyes once more to the far bank. The shadows had stopped moving. Their figures had blended in with the darkness, and as the greyish blueness of the evening had given way swiftly to night, they had become completely unnoticeable. Berfrand couldn't tell whether they were there anymore.

"Do you think we've been followed?" he asked, turning to Dragan. His friend's blue eyes tensed.

"No, I can't imagine we have. We took off abruptly. The official royal schedule has us sailing two weeks later. If not for Yasna's desire to travel home, we would've still been with Mezamir."

"Then It's either a coincidence that these horsemen are here, or—"

"—or," Dragan completed the sentence, "somebody on board informed them of our journey."

Shadows danced across the hull's planks. Several candles, all set on crates and barrels fastened with ropes, shimmered and swayed subtly with the rocking of the ship. The passengers stood in the center for the meeting. Besides the captain, the prince, and Berfrand himself there was Gellius, with the other merchants of his own guild following closely behind, and of course, Princess Yasna.

She was somewhat tall, as were all the members of the royal family. They were known for their stature and good, strong bodies. Their hair was almost universally a dark shade of brown, though their eyes were a deep, lively blue. Both the men and the women of that house were fain to wear their hair in long, wavy locks strewn over their shoulders. Yasna was clad in a long, flowing dress of white, fringed with blue and gold decorations. Her older brother Dragan, though, liked green and brown more, and he looked like a grim ranger clad in such robes and tunics rather than a royal prince. Their faces were exceedingly similar to one another: long, full, noble, and beautiful as though carved to the image of liveliness and stoutness. Though in their looks they were warm and earthly, unlike Berfrand whose piercing grey eyes, deeply set under his locks of light blonde, and pale visage unnerved regular men.

Standing between such noble faces, the merchant Gellius sank in his place ever more, and his merchant friends whispered among themselves behind him. Berfrand bowed slightly so as to avoid one of the crossbeams running between the hull's walls and stepped forward into the circle. Beside Zelimir there stood several officers, all clad in their blue gambesons and bearing longbows in their hands.

"…a traitor among us?" Zelimir grimaced and placed a hand on the hilt of his dagger.

"That's what I think," said Berfrand.

"What is this assumption even based on?" merchant Velar, one of Gellius' companions, spoke up abruptly. "We don't even know If we are truly being followed." The man's features tensed up and his small, rat-like eyes carefully traced the room. The large gap between his two front teeth accompanied his leer.

"I'm of the opinion that we are," Berfrand cut in. "These parts of Gragus we're sailing through are not heavily populated. We are currently in a transition zone between the realm of Ernedin and that of Dvaziga further north. I deem it unlikely that any passers-by would suddenly ride on the sheer banks of Gragus, least of all within our sights."

"Hmm…" Zelimir mumbled as he scratched the greying goatee on his chin.

"B-But, who do you think could come this close to us?" Merchant Gellius blurted.

"That's what I want to discover tomorrow morning, if possible," Berfrand answered and put his hand on his sword's hilt. He eyed each of the faces around him but felt only Yasna's chasing his own. *She was always unsubtle in her mannerisms. Too demanding, too conspicuous*, thought Berfrand. The twain locked eyes as the conversation went on.

"—the river narrows abruptly some distance from where we are. I reckon we'll have to contend with the riders if they try to draw close to us around there," Zelimir spoke.

"If that is so, I reckon we'll possess the numerical superiority over them," Prince Dragan added. "We have about a hundred and fifty able bodied, fighting men aboard. Our archers shoot far and well. We can deal with a few horsemen."

"I hope we can," Berfrand said, "but whoever sent those riders knew of our journey, and it's very likely, therefore, that the enemy knows of our numbers as well."

"You reckon they've brought more?" Dragan raised an eyebrow.

"I don't know. It is possible that they've brought more men, but it's also possible that an ambush awaits us where the river narrows down, regardless of the numbers." Berfrand noticed that Yasna had not stopped looking into his eyes as he finished his words.

What do you want, your highness? Any questions in your mind? Maybe you'd like to berate me like you used to when we were little kids? Berfrand wanted to blurt out these words. Yasna's eyes had grown judgmental, and she stared with an expressionless face. Berfrand knew this wasn't a good sign.

Or maybe you'd like to take this up-deck. A swordfight,

Your Highness? I'm sure Mezamir would be proud of his little sister!

Berfrand shook his head in confusion. As he grew disgruntled, so did his thoughts turn confused and disorganized. Sometimes he wished he could gather his spirits as quickly as ordinary men, and not deal with these intrusive sentiments.

"—either way, we'll have to figure out whether there's truly an informant among us," Dragan finished his sentence.

A wave of chatter reverberated among those gathered before all agreed to the precautions set by the prince.

The meeting ended, and the group scattered. Zelimir took his archers onto the top deck, Gellius his merchants to their quarters in the second deck. Just as Berfrand himself had turned around to leave, he felt a tug on his cloak from behind. Feeling frustration at the prospect of that encounter which he had preferred to avoid, he turned around.

"Yes, Your Highness. You wanted to speak to me?" he tried to remain expressionless. His Elven gaze could dishearten even the strongest of men, but he knew it had little effect on Yasna.

"Since when do you address me like that?"

"What do you mean, Your Grace?"

"You know exactly what I mean, Herwin!" she bleated, no longer keeping herself in check, willing to spill everything out.

"No, Yasna, I don't. The last we had spoken, I had notified you to not address me by my real name," Berfrand pulled his cloak back with a hard tug of his hand, freeing it from Yasna's grip. He was losing his composure.

"The last time we had spoken?" Her face turned ghastly, then swiftly she furrowed her brow, "—the last time we had spoken was four years ago, Herwin! Four years have passed

168

without a single word from you! Then you showed up months ago unannounced and haven't said anything to me since!"

Her blue eyes shimmered deeply. The fire on the candles danced rueless, and their light glazed her brown locks, turning her fair skin to a pinkish orange.

"I had made it clear that we should end our correspondence," Berfrand drew into himself as he spoke.

"Yes. After you had decided to leave and play hero someplace else. Do you have any idea how much my father missed you? You were like a son to him, and you left without a farewell."

"I can tell it was only Kazimir that missed me."

"Now you're being cruel!" Yasna folded her arms on her bosom. "Mezamir too, and Dragan, and the old man Nagrom…"

"And you?" Berfrand raised an eyebrow.

"I…" Yasna turned her eyes down. Her judgmental, angry expression had faded away.

"Just as I had guessed, young princess. I had told you years ago on the cusp of your youth: Such early passions are quick to fade. If you had but listened to me back then, you would've saved us both from such a shameful public scandal. Have you considered that I may have remained distant from your father's court for so long to assuage the rumors?" Berfrand explained. Yasna's eyes rose up with a peculiar gleam, laden with sadness and wonder.

Berfrand sighed deeply. "But what's done is done. I cannot change the past, and neither can you. Either way, I'll have to rest and make ready for the confrontation tomorrow."

The princess was completely silent. As Berfrand turned away and started towards the stairs, Yasna finally opened her mouth.

"Berf."

"Yes?" Berfrand halted.

"Don't play the hero, please; it never bodes well for you," she purred, her voice sounded worried.

"It's not up to me to decide what to do, Your Highness."

That night was restless. Despite pretending otherwise, the conversation with Yasna had summoned memories which Berfrand had long kept untended. And as he lay down to sleep, endless thoughts beleaguered his mind. The clouded stars had drawn a deep darkness over the land, and the shadows about the boat had deepened. In such a mood Berfrand lay for long on the main deck. About him, on their bedrolls strewn between the benches and on the walkways, slept the rest of the crew. The privileged passengers were given their own quarters in the decks below, but despite being offered a position there, Berfrand had declined. The last thing he wished was to be any closer to Yasna. He knew it would only provoke further confrontations.

The morning drew over the horizon; the skies turned bright blue, and the clouds were scattered like white brush strokes. The decks stirred with the calling, the shouting of men, the pulling of ropes, the handling of oars, the lapping of water beside the hull, and the mewing of gulls far above the sailless masts.

As time passed, Gragus narrowed gradually. The lands about them tended ever so gently upwards, and the banks on either side climbed higher and rockier. Large boulders

170

stood about the shores as the width between them decreased to a mere furlong. There were bushes and short, squat trees strewn about between the rocks on either bank, and they obscured the watchful eyes of the crew. For Berfrand's piercing sight, however, the horsemen riding behind those trees were conspicuous.

Berfrand had notified the officers, and the passengers were sent below deck on command. The oars were pulled back, shields were gathered, and quivers were set about the deck. On fore and aft castles stood a dozen archers, ready to rain arrows on the horsemen circling between the trees.

"They're approaching!" Dragan cried out.

"Careful! They might have archers among them!" Zelimir's voice resounded. He had donned his hauberk, and the helmets of the men about him gleamed like fire beneath the sun's light.

"Do you see who they are?" Dragan whispered to his friend.

"Grawlings," Berfrand answered, squinting to make out who their leader was.

"Grawlings? All the way on the shores of Gragus?" Dragan's brow rose in surprise.

Grawlings were raiders and murderers. Once men, they had been corrupted and turned into savages. Though cruel and backwards, they weren't stupid, and their ability to track the ship was a sign of their competence.

"Unusual to find them here, so far away from their eastern settlements." Berfrand noted.

"Do you reckon— that someone truly informed them?" Dragan asked.

"Not only that, I reckon someone *hired* them specifically

for this," Berfrand bit his lower lip in anticipation. The horse-men on the western bank were anything but savages. They were clad in leather and linen armour, with looted bits of mail and even splint worn by those better off. Their hands bore lances, bows and javelins, and about their belts shook their quivers and scabbards as their horses trotted up and down in an orderly fashion.

"What are they doing?" one of the archers called out.

"They're not attacking yet!" another one answered.

There were murmurs and whispers among the men as all eyes locked onto the horsemen. None dared to even blink. The water drifted the galley ever so slowly towards the bank.

Then there came a horrible shout.

"They're on the other shore!" one of the archers called out.

"Get down!" Berfrand cried out and hauled both himself and Dragan onto the deck floor. He had noticed the volley just in time. A shower of arrows hit the deck from the eastern side. The arrows twanged and cracked as some hit the hull; others found their targets and fell several crew members before they could turn around. Those quick to act had hidden behind their shields.

"Ready yourselves!" Zelimir roared. An arrow had plunged itself into his shoulder, but by the way he moved Berfrand could tell it hadn't penetrated his body.

"Shoot!" Zelimir roared again, and several archers fired back in succession.

A grim skirmish had begun. The deck was receiving volleys from both the eastern and the western sides, though the volleys were heavier from the east where the Grawling archers had gathered. The din of shouts, the straining of bowstrings, the creaking of the hull, and the heavy sound of arrows travelling through the air screened the background.

"How many are there?" Dragan groaned.

"Too many to count," Berfrand grumbled.

"More than our crew?"

"More."

The skirmish went on for what seemed like hours. On both sides there were warriors falling. Javelins and arrows flew above; some found their targets, and some did not. As men fell to arrow-volleys, the cries of the injured and the groans of those straining to shoot back filled the air. Berfrand had just taken a bow for himself when he spotted a horseman on the western bank. He was clad in heavier armour and seemed much better off than those who rode with him. Around his helmet was tied a simple cloth of red fringed with gold, symbolizing his status as chieftain.

Berfrand nocked an arrow, waiting for that pause between the volleys. Then he rose up suddenly and shot. The string twanged loudly, and the arrow hissed swiftly through the air. It caught the horse's throat right above the reins and plunged deep. The creature buckled on its front legs and turned over. Its rider tried to jump down from his saddle but failed miserably. He tumbled along with the horse. A dust cloud rose between the trees. The Grawling riders circled around their chieftain. Their voices, muffled by the din of battle, rose in their wicked, ugly tongue. Throwing shouts and bickering between them, they tried to raise their chieftain.

Noticing the confusion, the Grawling archers had paused their volleys. Noticing this in turn, the crew members cried in shouts of joy and shook their weapons. Beating their shields with their fists and weapons, they taunted the Grawlings. Over the water were hurled insults from both sides.

"Don't dawdle! Onto the benches you fools! Row away now!" Cried Zelimir. Berfrand noticed were two more arrows sticking out of his hauberk.

Startled out of their taunting, the men scuttled onto the benches. Officers replaced the dead rowers and lowered the oars. In the blink of an eye, the ship had started moving.

"Move, you dogs, row faster!" Zelimir cried out. In between bouts of rousing his men, he was trying to pick targets with the crossbow in his hands.

"Get down!" cried Dragan and pulled Berfrand on to the deck floor. Just as they had knelt, an arrow volley came diagonally over the deck and caught a number of the rowers. Cries of pain resounded across ship. Some were shot dead immediately and fell over their oars like bags of sand.

"Now I've repaid you!" Dragan grinned.

"Indeed," Berfrand smiled back, "but If we don't get out of this predicament fast, we won't be able to celebrate that fact."

Just in that moment, something else caught Berfrand's eye. The peering visage of Velar was scuttling about on the staircase leading onto the main deck. In the shadowed stairs, Berfrand caught a glimpse of the man's face. He was calm, almost knowing, too unusual for a merchant who had just caught a glimpse of the blood-strewn deck. And noticing that, Berfrand remembered that he had seen the man several times before during the haze of the skirmish. Every time, despite being warned by the officers and shouted off and shoved down the stairs, he had scuttled back, his rat-eyes peering out onto the perilous deck with their calm gaze.

"I think I might have an idea," Berfrand mumbled to himself.

"What?" Dragan blurted. They were kneeling, almost

lying on the floor.

"I think I have an idea who the informer is."

The fighting had stopped. Nothing but groans and the distant, softly echoing calls of gulls were heard. The Grawlings had stopped shooting as the galley had rowed itself onto the wider expanse of the river. Here, the fighting prowess of the Grawlings was halved as the foot archers on the eastern bank had remained out of range.

"Why did they accept?" one of the archers asked, raising his nasal helmet and wiping off the sweat above his brows.

"They must've lost a lot of men," Zelimir noted, "far too many to not hear our proposal." He was squinting, eyeing each horseman carefully. The Grawling chieftain stood leering on the western bank, and about him the horsemen had stopped trotting. The archers on the eastern banks had sunk behind rocks and trees, but the crew could see their helms at times gleaming under the sun.

For a while this stalemate continued, until the lamenting cries of a man were heard on the stairs from the lower decks.

"No, sir! Please don't throw me overboard! I swear— I'm innocent— sir, please!"
Berfrand emerged into the light of day, hauling behind him the merchant Gellius. He had seized the poor man by his collar, and, dragging him behind like a sack of grain, he forcefully pushed his way onto the deck.

"What are you doing?" Dragan blurted, but Berfrand dismissed his concerned friend with a gesture.

"Clever scheme, I must say!" He loudly proclaimed. The fat merchant he held was flailing around, trying to free himself in vain. The elf-man's grip was too strong, his stature and power too great.

"Clever scheme, our dear guest! King Kazimir terminated a very lucrative business, so you wanted to push his hand. Kidnapping two of his children would give you a huge chip for bargaining," Berfrand continued onto the side of the ship. The eyes of the crew were locked onto the figures on either bank. The Grawlings were quiet. Bringing the merchant onto the side of the hull, Berfrand held him threateningly on the edge.

"Zelimir! Shout to the Grawlings what I'm about to say!" Berfrand called to the captain. Zelimir nodded, not tearing his eyes away from the horsemen.

Berfrand began to shout his conditions one by one: "We have your patron seized. If you force our hand, we'll behead him right here!"

Zelimir shouted the same words over the water. The river was narrow enough so that voices could easily be heard on the banks.

"A duel shall be arranged. On a small boat will meet the Grawling chieftain and one from the crew. The duel shall be to the death!" Berfrand called out, and Zelimir transferred his words.

"Are you sure about this?" Dragan rushed to his friend's side. "They can shoot us even if we kill their patron," he added; his unsure eyes examined the whimpering merchant.

"I am. Grawlings are clever, but they can't function without a leader," Berfrand answered firmly, "if I take him out, then—"

"If that is so, then I should be the one to duel the chieftain," Dragan lowered his tone as he spoke.

"No, friend. I am the best swordsman on board, and that Grawling chief is no weakling based on what I can tell of his warband. He must be a respectable warrior if he was able to gather so many to his cause."

The mewling of Gellius was the only sound that screened their conversation.

"Even if that is the case—" Dragan moved closer and grasped his friend's empty arm. "—you're the last of the Hrokling line! I'm merely the second prince of Dvaziga. If you die in this duel, then your kingdom is lost!" Dragan whispered, trying to keep his voice lowered.

"If you die," Berfrand sharply uttered, "then Yasna loses her closest sibling. Your father loses a potential heir, and your kingdom loses a valuable warrior. My kingdom is already gone, friend. If I die here, it affects none."

"Stop being a fool!" Dragan was struggling to keep his voice low. His grip had become firmer. "Stop trying to—"

"I've said no, Dragan," Berfrand retorted sharply. "Stop trying to play the hero!"

The Grawlings had accepted the terms. A small boat was drawn up between the galley and the western shore, floating in equal distance to each. Two boats were being rowed slowly, steadily towards the one in the middle. On each stood two men, one rower, and one fighter.

"Please, sir. Let me go! I haven't done anything!" Gellius cried out. His mewling and begging wakened nothing but disgust in Berfrand as he was rowed slowly across the water.

"Sit down and shut your mouth!" Zelimir shouted and pushed the merchant onto one of the benches. The merchant sat down with a loud thump and gawk. None on board wanted to miss a moment of the fight. Their gazes were steely. Their lives depended on Berfrand's success.

As the Grawling chieftain stepped onto the boat in the middle, Berfrand eyed his features carefully. They were human, unmistakably so, but corrupted and twisted in a manner inconspicuous. His complexion was a sickly grey, and his skin looked like paper strewn over a wet surface, barely holding together. His eyes were set deep in his skull, and their whites had turned yellowish.

"How much did the merchant pay you?" Berfrand asked. He had left his cloak on the galley, and with only his sword he stepped onto the boat.

The Grawling grinned mischievously. "Not a single coin," his voice was raspy and deep.

"Then why are you here?"

"Somebody else sent us. You know of him already," the chieftain drew his scimitar slowly.

"I know of him?" Berfrand asked.

"Of course you do!" the chief cackled. His blade was completely out. Berfrand hadn't yet drawn his own.

"What does that person presume to gain from kidnapping Kazimir's children?" Berfrand gripped his sword slightly.

"Nothing, for we are not here for the princelings," the chief cackled again, this time followed by a muffled cough. The fall from the horse must have damaged his torso. But Grawlings were sturdy creatures, they would not give into wounds easily.

178

Berfrand's eyes widened in surprise. *Could it be?* He thought.

"We've come here for you, Berengar's son," the chieftain spilled his words, "and you've willingly cast yourself before me. For what, to play the hero? I will sever that straw head of yours from your shoulders, then take it to my master!"

A brief silence ensued. Berfrand heard nothing but the lapping of water on the boat's sides, and the mewing of gulls. He gripped the hilt tightly, and then broke the silence.

"If that is so, then rejoice! Your prey has arrived!" Before the chieftain had time to react, Berfrand was upon him.

The twain clashed their blades, and Berfrand's sword, Swintgilt, shone with a dim, pale light as it leapt out of its scabbard. The warrior swiveled around the chieftain; his movements were inhumanly agile, and jumping across the length of the boat he shifted his weight from one leg to the other. The Grawling barely had the time to react, and though he managed to block the strokes of Swintgilt, he was not swift enough to block all of them.

Berfrand's ire rose within him. This creature knew of his father. He knew of his home, and whoever had sent him knew of his lineage as well. The notion of there being someone who presumed the strength to hurt Berfrand, to try and hurt his friends, fanned the flames of his wrath. Like a wild wolf he leapt forward, and his blade slashed the air like a pale, falling star.

A loud slash echoed over the water. A head flew off far into the air and twirling down it plunged into the river. Blood spilled all over the boat from the wound, and the body which had once stood with a head lurched in its place like a doll.

"Farewell, fiend," Berfrand snickered and kicked the

headless corpse of the Grawling overboard. A loud swish accompanied the body as it first plunged into the river, then started floating amid small pools of black blood.

The crew couldn't believe how quickly the fight had resolved. Berfrand was too fast for their eyes. Realizing now what had happened, they broke suddenly into loud cries of joy and hails. Beating their shields and ramping their feet in unison. Berfrand turned to face the crew. The fight was over.

Just then, he felt a sharp sensation in his back. It was followed by another sharp pain just below his scapula. He felt his strength wither away immediately as though sucked by the two objects in his back. He saw the eyes of the crew afar fall dark. From joy to a horrible realization they were suddenly drawn. Their mouths opened in horror and rage, but there came no voice out of them. Berfrand stumbled forward. His body was still strong, but his legs were shaking. Unable to find his footing, he fell overboard and plunged into the blue waters of Gragus. As he sunk below, he could see arrows flying over the surface of the water.

Blue waters…
Blue sky…
Blue eyes…
Blue…

He was startled out of his deep sleep by the creaking of wooden planks. A dull ache pulsed in his temples. Instinctually, he wanted to sit on his bed, but as he moved up, he felt the sharp pain of the two wounds in his back. His clothes were
180

gone, and his torso was wrapped in white cloth. His eyes took a while to adjust to the light around him. At once he sensed a pair of soft arms hugging his neck. A gentle, worried moan graced his ears, and he felt the tickling of brown locks about his face and chest.

"He's finally awake!" cried Zelimir. "It took a while to drive out the Grawlings, but thanks to him we've managed."

"Indeed," nodded Dragan, "not much of a match when leaderless."

They were in the lower deck, and Berfrand had been settled into a thick bedroll. Two candles were set on the barrels near them, and above him he saw the looming faces of the crew.

"What did I tell you?" Yasna released her hug on Berfrand. "Didn't I tell you to not play the hero?"

Berfrand groaned in pain. There were mumblings and laughs in the small crowd that had gathered about his bed.

"No use saying it to a man like him," Dragan cackled out his words.

"Indeed," the crew physician added from the back. "His wounds were already healing when I stitched him up. Unbelievable how lucky he is."

"It wasn't luck," Berfrand finally spoke. His voice had turned raspy as though he had slept for a long while. He still saw the grin of that Grawling chief in his mind, and he heard his raspy voice uttering his father's name.

"Of course it wasn't luck!" exclaimed a generous, high pitched voice from among the group. Only then did Berfrand realise Gellius had been standing near him. His face was strangely friendly despite what had occurred.

"Merchant Gellius, I-I'm sorry for what had occurred. I thought it was—" Berfrand stuttered, trying to apologise.

Shielding his eyes from the bright candles with one hand, he tried to look up.

"Of course it wasn't me!" The merchant exclaimed, rubbing his hands together.

"The informer jumped overboard during the duel," Zelimir stated. "He was one of the other merchants."

"That rat, Velar," Gellius furrowed his brow as he spoke and shook his fist, "I'll get him when the time comes for putting me in danger like this."

An image of that merchant who had scuttled about the stairs flashed in Berfrand's mind. He had assumed the man was there by Gellius' orders.

"You shouldn't jump to conclusions like that, you know?" Dragan contorted his lips into a peculiar smile. "It doesn't bode well for you."

"I know," Berfrand hawked deeply from the pain of his wounds. "And neither does playing the hero."

The Bizarchives

The Statement of Carter Brinton
by Froskaz

I spotted it one day, seeping through the carpet in my study. I was quite shocked at first. I keep a pristine home and have a tendency to walk around barefoot, so I certainly would have known if it was damp. Besides, I never brought food or drinks into this room, consuming them only in their proper place at my dining table.

To tell the truth, I have never been a forgiving man. I was infuriated that such an excellent carpet would be ruined by such a thing! I could not think what might have caused it, for I had several friends that all had much worse houses than mine that didn't have these kinds of problems. I knew this for a fact, as I had called each one and inquired about it specifically after it had occurred. I then sent my landlord an email describing the situation but assured him that I would be the one to take care of it, and I was simply informing him prior. It would not help at all to have such a grubby man in my own home after all – who knows what he might bring in? He had been here recently, and it had not been a pleasant experience to say the least. No, the less involved he is the better, I thought, and after doing so I set about researching how to remove the vile infection, lest it spread.

It seemed simple enough, requiring only protective gear – disposable isolation suit, goggles, gloves, and an effective face mask (all of which any prudent homeowner should already have), some baking soda, vinegar, and a vacuum cleaner with a particularly capable filter. It should not be too hard, I thought, since the room was mostly empty except for an old wooden desk and chair combination at the far end. I set the baking soda down on the affected area and left it overnight, though my instincts wished that I would ignore the proper procedure and remove that repulsive stain on my otherwise immaculate household.

But leave it I did, and the next day I scrubbed the carpet roughly with a vinegar-soaked brush. This allowed me to get close to, and glare vehemently at, that disgusting fungus that threatened to permeate my home. It came off easily and in layers of milky white strands. I frowned at this. Though this was my first encounter with any variant of carpet mould, I was still somewhat educated in the biological sciences, and this did not feel quite right. However, many real things in this world have exceeded my imagination, and, after all, that education was many years ago. Part of me was tempted to properly analyse it just in case it truly was some unknown type of fungus, perhaps getting the chance to name it and thereby contribute to science in my own way. But those feelings were overwhelmed by my desire to remove it from my abode and be done with the disgusting thing.

After vacuuming it up, I put it in a plastic bag and put it in the outside bin, feeling once again secure within my own home. The next day I came downstairs and almost went into a fit of rage! That damned fungus had repopulated the previously cleaned sections and more! I must have missed a spot, though I was sure that I hadn't, and went around manically, hurling baking soda at and over the entire carpet and then frantically checked my watch every ten minutes until six hours was up. There was no chance that I would wait a whole 'nother day! Although, some reasonable and soft part of me had piped up and conceded that I should wait at least some amount of time, and so six hours it was.

I went at it with the vinegar brush like a mad butcher, removing and then hoovering the mould as quickly as I could. Only when I was sure I had got everywhere did I go over it all again, and then again for a third time. Only after throwing it in the outside bin did I allow myself a moment of respite, before checking my watch and realising it had almost passed my dinner time. That wouldn't do, but luckily I was able to fix myself up some small sustenance in the time I had left.

The morning after, I had come downstairs early; woken by disturbing dreams I could not quite remember. All the stress must be getting to me, I realised, as I had not been stressed for some years. But many years' worth came to me all at once in that repulsive moment, as I stared in appalled horror at how the carpet of my study was absolutely covered with the milky white fibres. I slowly backed away, calmly putting on my protective gear and drawing a knife from its holder in the kitchen, the largest one I could find. Coating the knife in vinegar, I deliberately walked to the carpet. In an instant I fell upon it as a beast, ripping and tearing and stabbing and mauling and slicing until my arms ached and my heart pounded. I surveyed the damage around me, carpet and mould strewn everywhere. The rug was already done for. I had decided that when I first saw it earlier, despite its age and brilliance. It had been thoroughly corrupted, and it had to go, and so I gave it no quarter.

Sitting down and breathing heavily, I absentmindedly picked up a piece with a gloved hand. I was not sure which side was the top and which side was the bottom, at some point in all the madness I had realised that the mould was on both sides, and even covered the floorboards!

That was likely why it kept growing back. I looked at the piece further, and something more occurred to me. With my knife, I slowly dissected it until the truth became apparent. The mould was inside the carpet. Not just buried inside, but somehow fused deeply with the material of the carpet, in a way I could not understand. Tossing the knife to the ground, I hurried back up to my feet and gave my study a full appraising look. Wandering out, I headed down to the garden shed. I had bought all the necessary tools but scarcely used any of them, except to keep up to neighbourhood standards. I picked up a thin shovel and gave it a few testing thrusts. It would do.

Once back in my study, I brought it down into the floorboards again and again and again, until they had smashed into several pieces. I looked at the wood and found the same strange occurrence; it had somehow made its way through the wood itself without causing damage. I shuddered at the thought that it might infect my entire home in much the same manner before too long.

I once more composed myself, and turning to the closest wall, swung again. The wall shards showed the same thing, though on a smaller scale. Though there was very little on the outside, the mould had already begun to burrow through, which had become obviously visible when looking from the side. How was this possible? None of the wood had been eaten out, and it seemed to my eyes that it was as if the mould had superimposed itself on the wood. A shiver went through me as I realised how difficult it would be to remove. I stared at it once more, this time vindictively and full of hate. I

188

tossed the wood back on the ground, and stormed out of the room, slamming the door behind me. This was getting far beyond me. This would undoubtedly require more specialised help and arranging that was the landlord's domain.

I hesitated only a few minutes before calling him. Distasteful as he was, the situation in my study was far more so. He only picked up on the third call, somehow souring my mood further. After I explained the situation to him, he insisted I was overreacting and demanded I send a picture to him, although I dreaded returning into that room, even if only to look. But go in I did, and it seemed to my mind that the mould was growing, spreading, even right before my eyes. I sent him the picture and he was silent for quite a few seconds before telling me he would be over soon, with a certain edge to his voice. I felt pleased that, despite his other faults, at least he understood the gravity of the situation. Still, I felt more than a little impatient, and sat on a chair facing the study door, staring, almost challenging that damnable fungus to grow through.

I heard the key turn in the lock and could see the large form of the landlord through the patterned glass window that made up my door. I didn't get up to greet him, opting to keep an eye on my study. I simply called out a greeting to him as he entered, and he practically growled in response. I frowned. "You ingrate! What makes you think you can smash up my house?" he yelled, and I turned to see an almost-violet face barrelling towards me. At first, I was shocked. What was the idiot babbling about? The room was basically done for, we would be lucky if we could even save the house. Resentful that I actually thought such a person would be able to help, and already impatient, I retorted.

"Damn you! You small-minded fool, that fungus had already destroyed it!" He was leering over me by this point and given his height and mine I could not even see past his chin to glare back into his beady little eyes.

"What fungus?" he snarled. This made me pause. How could he not know? Then it clicked. Could he really be that much of an idiot, that he did not even understand the situation we found ourselves in? I had no time for uneducated men such as him, least of all when they seemed intent on making things difficult for me.

"The mould, you imbecile!" I half-screamed, rushing to the study door, flinging it open. He barged past me and angrily surveyed the room.

"Do you have any idea how much this is going to cost? I've never liked you, but I've always been fair. But you trash the place for a bit of mould, and you expect me to take it? Give me my money, and then get out."

"A bit? Damn you man, don't you see it all around you?"

"The only thing I see is a crackpot with a destroyed room!" he yelled, whirling around to face me. Now that I was about a metre from him, I could see his face clearly, and it froze me. His pupils contained those same fibrous streaks of milky white running through them, and now that I looked, I could properly see them running just underneath his red skin, like some twisted facsimile of veins. I paused, and time seemed to slow as my brain raced, frantically collecting my thoughts. Everything made sense now, far too much sense, a horrible sense. Trying to force myself to sound calmer than I was, I started to speak, gesturing vaguely to the hole behind him.

"…No, I mean it is in the walls. You have to look inside the walls to see it. Then it becomes obvious." He just stood there, looking at me coldly. Did he suspect me? Had the vile thing corrupted his brain as well as his eyes? For a moment I thought he was not going to move, but then he began to turn,

190

and marched over to the wall. With his gaze off me, I slowly bent down and reached for the knife I had dropped in my earlier assault on the carpet. Without my mask, the smell of the vinegar was almost overpowering as I brought it close to me. The landlord's face was turned away from me, halfway buried in the wall.

"I don't see anything in here," he muttered, though he didn't sound sure of himself. Before he could begin turning back to me, I lunged. Falling upon him with bloody savagery, I tore at his throat and his ghastly milky white eyes with my free hand, the other plunging the knife in him all over from his legs to his ribs to his back to his neck, and he clawed and scrambled and bit and swung his fists at me with equal vigour.

Eventually he began to slow down, and my knife found purchase more and more often. I slashed and plunged the blade into his arms and his body as I could, in every way I could, even using it as one would a chisel to force it through the hard plates of his skull. I had to be thorough.

He screamed like a pig throughout all of it, his wails reaching an unearthly and appalling pitch, but I didn't stop for a second, even when I knew the job was done. Finally, with sharp, shuddering breaths I took a moment of respite, allowing myself to think clearly once again. Raising my knife again in defiance of my aching shoulders, I sliced him wide open across the stomach, so his intestines flowed out, and sure enough within the blood and the muck and the organs where the repulsive fungus had taken hold, I saw the same strands flowing through it all. His blood was more white than red, and his organs were coated thickly in the fibres. I ripped at them, pulling them out, wishing that I might free him of that disgusting organism.

That was where the police found me. They grabbed me

191

roughly and shoved me against the floor. I yelled and screamed and sobbed at them to remove the mould as I was taken away, but they only told me that they did not see anything.

After that, the proceeding trial was a blur. I only remember that they brought forth the picture I had sent to my landlord, and I begged and pleaded with them to see what I saw but was once again told that there was no mould there, or white marks of any kind.

I do not know where I ended up, be it prison or a mental institution. It matters very little, for I am in a prison worse than any human making, as I am trapped in a room infested by the mould. I know who brought it here, too. For not long after the police had shoved me onto the floor of my study, I could feel it start to grow first on me and then within me. I could see it before long also, insidiously making its way throughout my whole body. There is now not one part of me not afflicted with it, from my brain to the soles of my feet. I tried to tear it out, when I first felt it, but a group of guards came in and strapped me to my bed. They claimed it was for my own protection. They could not know it was the opposite! I have tried to kill myself as to stem the damnable growth, but after I first attempted to remove the fungus, they keep me on watch and do not allow me anything capable of doing the job.

How I cursed and raged at them impotently, that I alone might have prevented the advancement before it had me completely. I do not know that it controls me, or even does anything to me, but why should it have to? Any good parasite will not instantly kill its host, else it will not be able to spread. I do not even think it's sentient, as I once suspected, but that it is no more aware than the common mould. I think it must be guided by some instinct at least, for only once it had done with me did it start to spread to others. The guards that had touched me, the bed I lie on, it even burrows through the very walls around me, the stone and the steel. Nothing can stop it, and I still do not understand how it works, I cannot comprehend it!

Its infestation never seems to eat through anything, it somehow inhabits the same space as it, joining it up to the same mass of seething white strands. Occasionally, I can see it, feel it, swaying and undulating ethereally, as if in response to some unknown and ghastly wind. Whether it be a cosmic invader or something from a different dimension, I do not know, but nothing so nightmarish and repellent could have spawned from the same Earth that conceived us.

I know it can be removed, though, and brought forth to the physical. I know not which element of my cleaning apparatus worked on it, though I suspect it was the vinegar. But this truth does me no good. This place is already so infected, and I see it growing every day, throughout the building, and even in the people I see out of my lonely window. The ones with visitors unknowingly pass it to them, and the ones who leave could take it to any corner of our planet.

I can feel this whole area, through the mould I am connected to, and it is a disgusting and appalling sensation that human minds were never meant to conceive; even now my mind threatens to rupture, and occasionally I go into feverish fits of ataxia as I forget myself within that febrile mass.

From my observations I do not believe it affects other humans as it affects me, and I am sure they cannot feel me as I feel them, the whole of them, through the perspective of fibres of milky-white mould.

What's worse, I sometimes feel their thoughts and desires, and more recently, I have come to feel the mould's desires. It seeks only to connect to the other parts, and it brings me to weeping as I consider the new alien and repulsive perceptions I will undoubtedly be subjected to when this occurs. Occasionally, I wonder if even death would release me, or whether I will forever be forced to play the part of the marionette now that it has me.

The blight spreads so fast and so totally that I cannot help but wonder when the whole earth will be consumed and become little more than a disgusting giant fungal outgrowth, and I fear what terrible vistas of reality it might then connect to. Whatever twisted realm this thing comes from, I do not wish to know it but fear it is inevitable that I will. I shudder to think of it and wish sorely that my end comes first.

I release this document, first and foremost, as a confession and a warning. I should have tried to study the fungus, or contain it, or tried to find a method to save some of humanity, even if it would have only been small portions. As it stands, I know no one will believe me, save those that might be able to see it as I have, and I hope they will be able to save themselves.

But for the rest of us, I know it is far too late. I know that even if the whole of humanity acted instantly and in unison, it might still be far too late. And so secondly, I can ask only for forgiveness for my own role in this, as our very world becomes infected and forced to become little more than a tainted host for this vile thing.

The Bizarchives

The Sound from Beneath: An Homage Properly and Lovingly Crafted
by C.J. Miller

I cannot say with any degree of certainty when first the dreams began, but of late I have begun to suppose that they have been with me my whole life, and it is only recent events which have caused me to recall them.

But allow me to start at the beginning – or at least, at the day on which this whole strange affair of the last few weeks developed. I had only just recovered from a brief bout of fever, which had left me bedridden for two days, and was feeling restless. I decided to take a walk around the grounds of the family estate to restore some vigour to my body.

The Phillips Estate on which my family has lived and died for the last three hundred years is modest in size compared to the enormous commercial farms which have surrounded and encroached towards the edges of our once-secluded property over the last century, yet still large enough, as I have discovered, to conceal its own secrets.

I set out from the manor house that evening in a jovial mood, rejoicing, as one does after a period of illness and confinement, in the fresh air and the freedom of my own body. I walked much longer than I normally would, right to the edge of our property, and from there took a circuitous route approximately following the property line, which finally brought me, as the last of the evening light faded, along the dark and densely wooded area near the furthest corner of our estate, far behind the manor house.

In the early days of the estate, my ancestor H. Phillips had cleared the woods here up to the edge of the property to sow crops, but successive generations had found that nothing would grow in the area and attributed the cause to some unwholesome quality of the soil. A well had been dug here as well, with which to water the crops during dry periods, and it had been used for several decades, being dug deeper and deeper, until one year the water had developed a noxious odour and turned poisonous to the plants.

Since then, both the bad well and the attempts to sow a field had been long abandoned, and the dark woods had crept back onto our estate, reclaiming all the earth from which H. Phillips had forced them back. In just a couple centuries, the trees had already become remarkably thick, their canopy heavy and dark, their roots and branches gnarled and twisted. Like so many other things around the estate during the reign of my father, whose incessant drinking consumes nearly all his attention and who is stubbornly uninterested in the heritage and history of our family, the entire area for several acres around had fallen into a sorry state of disuse and disrepair. Since there was now neither well nor field here, this corner of our estate was almost never visited after those early attempts to make use of it. The woods on our northern border were still old and wild, and for generations the women of our family had always warned their children and grandchildren not to go into them.

What compelled me, then, to walk here on that evening I could not say at the time. The obvious answer would seem to be that I was simply following the natural course along the boundary of our estate, and so I thought as well at the time. But after my recent experiences, I wonder whether it was not something quite outside myself which called me there.

The twilight grew dim as I neared the treeline. By the time I was a stone's throw from the edge of the woods, the sun had dipped below the horizon, and the shadows of dusk were chasing all the light out of the land. The waxing moon appeared above the horizon, and the cold sunlight that reflected from it gave the whole scene a pale, blueish hue and threw long, twisted shadows at the feet of the thick trees.

I was about thirty feet away from the edge of the woods, and just altering my course slightly to take me back along the boundary of the estate and back towards my starting point, when I first heard it – or perhaps I should say felt it. It was not that I heard it clearly or suddenly; rather, the sensation crept up on me gradually. As I walked roughly parallel to the treeline, I became aware of a giddy sensation, a sort of tingling that seemed to come upwards through my feet and affected my entire body. For a minute or so I ignored it, attributing the cause simply to my newly restored health, but as I walked, the odd feeling became more insistent. At some point I realised, too, that the strange sensation was indeed accompanied by a sound. Every time I felt the vibrations pass upwards through my body, I sensed a very deep, scarcely perceptible thrumming noise. I could not make out where it came from, as it seemed to fill the air around me, coming from everywhere at once. The sensation only grew more intense as I walked. I decided to pause a moment, steadied my breath, and strained my ears to try to determine its source. I continued to feel the vibrating sensation coinciding with the sound. There it was, every minute or so, a long, low pulse lasting several seconds, then a period of silence, followed by another deep pulse.

I walked on, and the sound grew more intense. The strange quality of the moonlight gave the twisted trees a grotesque resemblance to human bodies contorted in agony. Somewhere close, I knew, was the bad well, swallowed up by the dark woods. I stopped again and tried to peer into the impenetrable darkness of the growth, hoping to catch a glimpse of the well and wondering whether the sound might be coming from inside of it – underground water flowing, perhaps, or even tectonic plates shifting. It was far too dark and the woods too thick for me to see the well at the time, but I have since learned that I was standing almost in front of it, only about twenty yards away.

I took another step towards the woods and felt the pulsing sound again, so deeply and powerfully that its subsonic vibration nearly buckled my knees. Another step forward, and the next pulse came seconds later, even deeper than the first, then the pause. My heart began to flutter wildly, and I felt a fear and fascination unlike anything I can possibly explain to you. I froze, rooted to the spot. The hairs on the back of my neck stood on end and my flesh broke out in goosebumps in anticipation of the next set of pulses. They came, resonating through every cell of my body, making my stomach lurch and my balance weak. I could not think straight.

After the last one subsided and the familiar pause ensued, a bizarre but insistent thought entered my mind: the sound resembled a heartbeat. It was inhuman, obviously, and had such an impossibly slow and strange rhythm as to seem not

200

quite natural, even, but the resemblance was unmistakable. I was filled with an indescribable sense of dread and awe, so overwhelming that every instinct urged me to run as fast and far as possible to save myself, and yet at the same time, an emphatic inner voice – which at the time I attributed to my own curiosity – told me to remain. I stood still and silent, not daring even to breathe, waiting for the next set of pulses, the next unearthly heartbeat.

The sound welled up from beneath me, passed through me, overwhelmed me, my mind swam with vague and bizarre visions and a feeling of impending doom, and I lost my consciousness entirely.

I must have been out there until late in the morning. The next thing I knew, I woke up in my own bed, groggy and disoriented, with my father and mother standing over me, peering anxiously at my face.

As soon as I awoke, my mother swarmed me with a flurry of concern and questions, none of which I was able to answer. I was barely able to register what she was saying and could only shake my head and try to wave her off. Vague, half-forgotten fragments of my dreams from the night before intruded into my mind, visions of a deep hole near the woods on our estate by the old well, accompanied by a deep-seated sense of unease. The images were strange and yet seemed somehow familiar, as though I had seen them before, long ago.

It took several minutes for me to regain my faculties fully. My mouth was dry, and my tongue felt hot and itchy.

"Water. Need water," I managed to croak weakly.

My mother stood again from her chair and began frantically calling for the servant to bring water, then crowded me again, demanding to know what had happened and why I had gone out at night.

My father stood then, placing a calming hand on her shoulder, and shushed her gently.

"Calm yourself, woman, and give the boy some space. He'll explain himself as soon as he's had something to wet his throat."

She stood back reluctantly, and just then a house boy knocked politely at the open door, holding a large glass of water balanced on a serving tray. My mother strode briskly across the room and snatched the glass from him, berating him for his sluggishness. She came back to my bedside and held the glass gently to my lips for me to drink.

I drank deeply, draining the whole glass in one go.

Mother stood back again and looked at me expectantly.

"Well? Are you going to tell us what you were doing out there, young man? You had your father and me scared nearly out of our wits!"

"I'm sorry, mother, but I have little idea of what happened myself. I went out for a walk in the evening after supper, you'll recall, and I must have fainted at some point. I suppose I was not as fully recovered as I had thought."

By then I had more or less remembered all the events of the night before leading up to my loss of consciousness, but the whole memory had such a bizarre and nightmarish quality that I was not even sure whether it was real, and decided to make no mention of the sound coming from underground near the old well.

My mother seemed satisfied with my explanation, though still concerned for my wellbeing. My father, though, eyed me with what almost seemed like suspicion, and I wondered whether he might suspect that I had left something out.

Still, he outwardly accepted my answer and explained to me that when I had not come back from my evening stroll long after dark, mother had begun to worry. When they had checked my bedchamber early in the morning and found that I had still not returned, they had sent everyone in the household out to search the grounds of the estate. It had been an old manservant named Reeves who had found me far from the manor house near the dark woods.

Again I explained to them that I had merely been strolling with no aim in mind, following the boundary of our property, and must have fainted due to the exertion so soon after my illness.

For the next couple of days everyone seemed largely to forget the whole incident, though on a few occasions it seemed that my father was eyeing me with a squinting, penetrating look. I ignored it, figuring the old man was simply too deep into his cups, which was often the case. As for myself, I did my best to go back to normal, and I didn't go near that far corner of our estate again. I did still think of the strange visions I had dreamt and was unable to shake the feeling that I had seen the same images before, but they grew increasingly difficult to recall, and soon I was no longer certain what had been a dream and what had really happened.

Then one night the dreams came to me again. In this dream, my vision seemed to float, disembodied, towards the place where I had fainted a few days before. The scene looked the same: the pale bluish moonlight, the densely overgrown woods – I could even hear the same sound which I was increasingly inclined to think of as a slow, impossibly deep heartbeat, and could feel its reverberations passing through me.

But here, as in the last dream, was a hole in the ground at the very place where I had stood when I fainted, leading straight down into the ground. I remember experiencing in the dream the same queasy sense of foreboding I had felt when I was really there, and I did not want to go near the hole; I desired nothing more than to run as far away from the place as I could. Yet at the same time, I felt drawn inexorably towards it. The sound was intense and insistent, and I could not turn away. I was pulled towards the hole, even as I struggled futilely against it, and when I looked down into it, deep down at the bottom I saw a circular barrier, something like a trapdoor. It seemed to be made of some queer stone whose ghostly colour perfectly resembled the hue given off by the pale moon, and it was carved around the edge with some sort of hieroglyphs whose design was completely alien to me. As I studied them, the overpowering sense of dread grew ever stronger, and yet with morbid fascination my vision followed their inscription around the edge of the doorway.

I could make nothing of most of them, but at the bottom of the circle was carved what appeared to be a grotesque and shocking depiction of some horrifying creature, which a religious man might have described as demonic. The thing was almost impossible to describe due to its bizarre and uncanny shape – something half-resembling the sea monsters that used to adorn old maps, perhaps, vaguely octopod and distinctly unearthly. Even the small and crude likeness was enough to make me recoil with abhorrence, yet paradoxically something about its abnormal form fascinated and enthralled me.

From the other side of that strange, glyph-carven portal, the sound called to me. It surged up from far below, causing the very ground to tremble and the stone of the door to thrum along to its frequency, until suddenly the door split open with an ungodly groan, like the mouth of a predator, inviting me to descend.

And then I awoke. I launched myself up from my bed into a sitting position, throwing the cold, sweat-soaked sheets from me in a moment of blind panic. I steadied my ragged breath, and as I calmed and quieted, I became aware of the sound again, faint but quite distinct, reaching me even at this distance of over a mile and through the stone walls of the manor house. I sat there silently, listening to the weird heartbeat and remembering with mingled unease and fascination the strange vision I had seen.

The hole in the ground had not been there in reality when I had happened upon the place during my stroll a few days before; of that I was quite certain. But the images of the dream had been so vivid, and the feelings so intense, and all of it so strange and yet somehow so familiar, that I felt it must have had some sort of significance. The peculiar round door I had seen with the hieroglyphs upon it – I shuddered at the mere recollection of that unsettling carving of that creature, even as the memory of its exact appearance grew vague in my mind – what if it really was there, and I had somehow missed it? Although, in my dream it had appeared in good condition, almost unscathed, in fact; it had given me the impression of being ancient, far older than the family estate. So, who could possibly have built it? Could the Red Indians who occupied this land long before us have created something with that level of workmanship? And if so, to what purpose? What could it lead to?

That I was even asking myself such questions was unusual, as I am normally inclined to consider myself a sceptic and have no interest whatsoever in the occult or supernatural, let alone any supposed meaning hidden in dreams. Nonetheless, I was unable to dismiss my morbid curiosity or calm my growing restlessness. Besides, the sound I was hearing and the reverberations it created through my body were all too real. I felt compelled, almost against my will and certainly against my better judgement, to go back to that place at the far edge of the estate and have another look, if only to assure myself that what I was hearing was simply the result of my imagination and perhaps some lingering effect of my recent illness.

To that end, at an ungodly hour of the night, I arose from my bed, hastily pulled on an old frock coat which had belonged to my grandfather and a pair of boots, took the gas lantern from my bedside table, and crept out of the house.

The night was cool but bright, even brighter than the first time I had gone out to that place. As I stole out a seldom-used back door of the manor house, the odd idea occurred to me to stop at the nearby garden shed and take a shovel with me. I did this with hardly a second thought as to why I might need it, so drawn by the penetrating sound and my own fateful curiosity that I could think of little else.

And so, with lantern in hand and shovel slung over my shoulder, I strode determinedly towards the treeline in the distance. I must have walked with unusual speed and vigour, for in what seemed like no time at all I was already near the woods.

The sound, of course, grew much louder as I approached, so that I could very likely have guided myself to the exact place with my eyes closed, using only its growing intensity to find the way.

I deliberately slowed my pace as I neared the place where I had fainted last time. The moon was more than half full now, and its queer, pale light revealed more to me. When I peered into the dark woods I could even dimly make out the shape of the bad well, only just visible through the trees. It was overgrown with bushes, gnarled roots had penetrated through at its base, and its old stones were covered with slimy black moss. A shiver crawled up my spine and settled in the nape of my neck at the sight of it, and my previous sense of unease returned in full force. I was hesitant to go any closer to the place where I had fainted, but it seemed silly to have come all this way only to go back without knowing any more than I had when I left my bed. Besides, as always seemed to be the case lately, my curiosity outweighed my fear, and I felt inexplicably drawn towards the source of the heartbeat.

I took a halting step forward, then another. My flesh crawled, and my thoughts became confused; the only thing that was clear to me was that this was where I needed to be, and I had to press on. One more step and I was standing right where I had last time. The sound called out to me, thundering up from beneath and washing every remnant of logical thought from my mind.

I knew then what I must do. I planted the blade of my shovel in the earth and began to dig. The ground was cold and hard, but I drove the blade deep into it and levered out huge chunks of earth, again and again, with a tireless energy and strength I had never known myself to possess. My progress was so fast that I was waist-deep before I realised it, then chest-deep. The sound grew ever louder, urging me on to new heights of strength and determination.

To anyone who saw me I would have appeared extremely suspicious, if not outright insane, but I did not think of that until much later. I could think of nothing at all, not even what I was doing. My body simply went through the motions of digging, and the only thing that my mind registered was the slow, steady DOOOM... dooom of the heartbeat far beneath my feet. It soon became unbearably intense, reverberating through the very core of my being, until again it overcame me and my world went black.

When my family noticed me missing, this was the first place they looked. Flabbergasted manservants hauled me out of the hole I had dug and carried me, still unconscious, back to my bedchamber, where I awoke.

I was alone in the room when I regained consciousness and had a little time to reflect on my strange experience before inevitably being bombarded with questions, concern, even outrage. I could hardly account for my own bizarre and entirely uncharacteristic behaviour, but for the moment that seemed to matter little.

What strange visions I had seen in my dreams! I had seen the hole again, much deeper than I had been able to dig it in reality, all the way down to that long-forgotten, glyph-carven door. This time the door had stood open, ready for me, beckoning, and beyond its mouth was a steep stair carved of the same queer stone as the door, leading endlessly downwards into impenetrable darkness. The heartbeat sounded clearer than ever, and I knew with absolute certainty that if I were to descend the stair I would find its source. The idea was both tantalising and terrifying. My instincts had told me to run, but an importunate part of my mind had urged me to descend.

A knock sounded at my door then, rousing me from my musing, and my father entered, stern-faced and solemn, followed by my mother, clutching a handkerchief and wringing her hands in anxiety. Wordlessly, my father pulled a chair up to the side of the bed for each of them and helped my mother settle into hers. She opened her mouth to speak but he raised a hand and silenced her.

"Would you care to explain yourself, boy?" he asked me resignedly.

"Please forgive me, Father, Mother," I began, formulat-

208

ing an excuse as I spoke. "I realise how strange this must seem. But you see, it is strange to me as well. I have only the vaguest memory of how I got there, and no memory at all of having dug a hole. The only explanation is that I must have walked there in my sleep." I could hardly explain my own actions, but I felt compelled to keep the heartbeat and the visions a secret all to myself.

"But why on earth would you have walked there?" interjected my mother. "Why would you go back to that horrid place?"

Again my father silenced her with a wave of his hand. "Sleepwalking, eh? I suppose that explanation would suffice. Sleepwalking is not unusual; you did it when you were a boy. What puzzles me most, though, is the sleep-digging."

"I do apologise, father, but I can hardly imagine what might have possessed me to take up a shovel in my sleep."

"What possessed you, indeed?" he mused, and I thought there was a subtle but distinct emphasis in his voice when he said possessed, an oddly suspicious tone that I did not much like. The way he studied me, as well, was peculiar: something in his eyes appeared mistrustful, and I was no longer sure that it was merely due to his drinking.

"I suppose it makes no matter, though," he continued at length, "for if you were indeed sleepwalking, then it is not as though you chose to wander out there of your own volition, is it?"

"Not at all," I answered, not breaking from his stern and guarded gaze.

"Still, I think certain measures are called for. The last thing we need is for some loose-tongued house boy to go gossiping about all this and bring embarrassment upon the family."

It occurred to me that his own fondness for the bottle was a far more likely source of gossip and embarrassment than anything I could do, but I held my tongue.

"You will no longer wander the estate alone," he continued, "especially not along the far boundary of the woods. And we will post a servant to sleep in the hallway outside your door at night to prevent you from sleepwalking into some lurking danger and harming yourself. Won't we, dear?" he said authoritatively, turning and addressing my mother.

"But of course! And you must promise, son, you simply must promise not to go near that place anymore!"

"You have my word, unreservedly," I promised them.

With a few more words which I don't recall, they finally seemed to be satisfied and left me in peace.

For the next couple of days I tried my best to return to my usual mode of life. I did not break my promise: I never wandered the estate, and never went near the woods and the bad well. My promise was easy enough to keep during the daytime; it was at night that I felt the call most strongly.

The first night I could hardly sleep. I lay awake for hours tossing and turning restlessly, and whenever I lay perfectly still and silent, I could hear the ominous heartbeat faintly but clearly, far away and deep underground.

When I finally fell into a fitful sleep, I was plagued by the most vivid nightmares, or perhaps I should say I was shown the most fantastic visions; I was no longer sure what to call them. My dreaming mind drifted over the land quite beyond my control, pulled towards the same place that drew me to it all the time. I saw the deep hole, the open door waiting for me, and my mind took me through that dark portal and began the descent down the steep, interminable stair. The heartbeat's echo boomed off the stone walls. I drifted down the stairs for what seemed endless hours, through the dense, almost palpable gloom.

The last visible streaks of wan moonlight had been left behind long ago and far above; now the only visible light was a very dim, almost imperceptible glow coming from the pale bluish stone of the stair. The deeper I went, the more my feelings of unease and aversion intensified into fear and outright panic until I was nearly hysterical. But the downward trek was entirely out of my control. For an impossibly long time the descent continued uninterrupted, punctuated only by the slow, abnormal rhythm of the heartbeat still far below. Though so intense it nearly filled my entire consciousness, the sound seemed to come from a great, deep distance, which led me to imagine that the stair truly had no end.

Thus it was rather unexpectedly that I came upon the cavern. The stair gave way quite suddenly to an immense, impossibly vast underground cave. The gloom was heavy and oppressive, and I could only vaguely make out its earthen walls and ceiling in the distant dark. The air felt warm and damp. The heartbeat, still coming from somewhere far below, echoed from everywhere at once. I was completely paralysed by fear. The malevolent and oppressive atmosphere was overwhelming, and my mind was almost in a blind panic, but I could neither run away nor wake up.

I had no choice but to remain where I was and scrutinise my bizarre and unnerving surroundings. Gigantic stalactites larger than bell towers hung menacingly from the ceiling, threatening like Damocles' sword. Some of their shapes bore a frightening resemblance to figures vaguely hominoid in shape, but quite unlike anything in the natural world. The entire cavern was bathed in a weird, greenish black light even dimmer than that of the stair. I searched the ceiling for its source but could only see the grotesque stalactites.

Only when I looked out at the floor of the cavern ahead of me did I discern the source of the unwholesome glow: an immense underground lake stretched before me nearly as far as my eyes could see. Its placid, ink-black waters were giving off the weird glow which, it then occurred to me, reminded me disconcertingly of the colour of putrefying flesh.

As I gazed out at the black lake with mingled fascination and horror, the heartbeat sounded again. Far in front of me on the noxious water, a giant bubble of air broke on the surface seconds after the sound, and for a fleeting, terrifying instant everything became quite clear to me, before my mind reeled and churned in a confusion of panic.

And then I woke up.

I was relieved to find myself in my own bed when I awoke. The sheets had been thrashed around and were piled and twisted up around my feet, and a cold sheen of sweat covered my skin, but I was not down in that impossible cavern – that was what mattered. I could no longer recall exactly what great revelation had come to me in the dream; I had only a vague sense of the enormous significance of it.

All that day I tried half-heartedly to put it all out of my mind, but if I was honest with myself, I was becoming less and less interested in putting on a façade of normalcy. When I tried to go about my day without thinking of the place, flashes of strange, unsettling imagery from my half-remembered dreams would intrude upon my mind and shake me to the core, and a sense of doom would come over me that made whatever chore I was engaged in seem entirely futile and meaningless. I did my best to conceal this from the rest of the

212

household – even the servants were not to be trusted, for the truth is that I have largely taken them for granted my entire life and have done very little to inspire in them any personal loyalty towards me; anything peculiar they observed in me was likely to be reported to my father and become the subject of gossip and speculation.

By the evening, I was increasingly overcome with distraction and restlessness to the point that I could not even bear to take my supper. I retired early to my bedchamber, citing nausea and weariness, and waited for sleep to take me again. At the time I actually thought that I hoped for a dreamless sleep, but I now realise that what I wanted was to see it all again, to be transported back under the earth and see the visions and find out what they meant. And in that regard I was not disappointed.

It seemed one moment I had closed my eyes in my bedchamber, and the very next I opened them in the immense underground cavern where I had been last night. The faint glowing light with the colour of disease and corruption was the same, and revealed to me that I was in the same place I had been last time. The tunnel of the long stair to the surface was behind me, but something in my mind – not my instincts, for those were still screaming at me to escape, but something else entirely – told me unequivocally that the surface was not to be my destination.

The sound boomed upwards from the deep, DOOM... dooom... and sure enough, a minute later a bubble of air rose to the surface of the lake. A shiver went through me, and a sense not merely of déjà vu but of destiny. I was called, and I would heed.

When my dream body began to float above the surface of the luminous ink-black water through no volition of my own, though I was afraid, I did not resist; this was what was supposed to happen, I knew it as surely as I have ever known anything. And when I reached the centre of the lake, floating there suspended for a moment, and then plunged headlong down into the water, though I was nearly overwhelmed by fear, I did not struggle against the force that drew me; I knew that to resist would have been pointless anyway.

Surprisingly, the water was comfortably warm. The dream was so vivid that I could feel it engulf my skin, but it did not fill my lungs or choke me. The murky blackness was impenetrable, and I could see nothing; I had only the sense that I was being drawn inexorably downwards, towards the source of the sound. As I descended, my mind's grasp on reality became more tenuous: first I forgot that I was dreaming, and then I forgot where I was, and next I forgot who I was.

That was when all was finally revealed to me. It was not with my eyes that I saw it all laid bare, but it was all much clearer to me than anything I have ever seen with my eyes open. I suddenly knew, with that knowledge that one has in dreams but whose source is mysterious, that the lake was unfathomably deep, and had been here for countless millennia, far beyond the measure of man. More importantly still, I knew the purpose of it all.

For at the bottom of that abysmal black lake lay the source of man's darkest nightmares, the primordial object of dread and worship for long-forgotten races, a being that I could not even begin to describe, vast beyond natural comprehension, unlike any living thing on earth, and ancient beyond earthly memory. Far beneath the ground, at the bottom of the dead lake, He had lain dreaming since long before time was counted.

I saw in a flash the entire history of this earth from the

time He had been here, æons passing before my vision in seconds, the entire history of man barely registering as a flicker. I knew an overawing dread and reverence, the intensity of which my previous fear and fascination had barely hinted at. And more dreadful and awe-inspiring still, I knew that it was time for Him to awaken.

My mind shrank and cowered from it all and gloried in the presence of the embodiment of Doom. For one disheartening moment of clarity, a mere fraction of a second, I knew that I was being driven to madness, just before my whole world was swallowed by darkness.

I awoke from this vision with a single-minded clarity of purpose that would have been the envy of any religious mystic. If only such men could see that they were on the wrong path entirely! I sprang from my bed with barely a thought in my mind and tip-toed across the floor to peer out the peephole in the door.

The old manservant Reeves had been stationed outside my door in the hallway as my father had promised, but he was fast asleep in his favourite armchair and snoring.

Ever so gently I turned the doorknob, painstakingly inched the door open, and crept across the hallway, down the staircase, and out a back door. This night the moon was nearly full and bathed the night in so much of its pale bluish light that I had no need for a lantern. I stopped at the garden shed to retrieve a shovel then made straight for my hole near the bad well that my ancestors had dug too deeply, too close to that cavernous hall beneath the earth.

As soon as I reached the place I jumped into the hole I had begun a few nights ago and set about my important work. Spadefuls of soil flew up from where I dug as the ground steadily gave way before me. I worked at a pace that under normal circumstances would have left me worn out and exhausted within minutes, but I never felt the slightest hint of weariness. In my trance-like state I dug down until the top of my head was below the surface, and I kept going, heedless of the time, of the tears in my muscles, of the bleeding blisters on my hands, which were admittedly unaccustomed to such labour. The heartbeat called to me from far beneath, reverberating upwards through the ground and into my very being, and I hastened to meet my destiny.

I could have kept going forever, and indeed, looking back on it, I believe I must have dug for several hours. I only stopped when, still digging in a manic frenzy, the blade of my shovel struck something hard. I squatted down, my heart fluttering with anxious excitement, my mind awash with nightmarish visions, and brushed at the dirt with my hands. The last thing I saw before I lost consciousness was a very faint glow, queer and pale, reflecting the strange light of the moon. The forgotten door was real, and I had reached it.

This time when they found me, the hole I had dug was so astonishingly and worryingly deep that a length of rope was required to haul me out. I was dressed only in my nightclothes, and my hands were a bloody mess, which caused my mother some consternation. The servants who pulled me from the hole were mystified as to how I had managed to get so deep, my mother was distressed, my father furious.

I did not care.

When they confronted me I made whatever noises I thought were warranted to make them leave me alone. I again offered the half-hearted and not very plausible excuse of sleepwalking, apologised without sincerity, and made my father a promise – which even then I never had any intention of honouring – to control myself and behave normally. I was far beyond caring what my father thought, that intemperate old fool. Even my mother, whose concern for me was genuine, I saw merely as an obstacle in the way of my destiny.

Reeves, the servant who had been ordered to watch me to make sure I did not leave at night, had been sacked when my father realised he had failed in his duties, which was rather unfortunate, as he had been with the family for his entire long life and had always served us loyally. But of course I knew that I was in no position to defend him. Besides, very soon it would not matter anyway.

My father ordered that I remain locked in my bedchamber the rest of the day and night until an expert psychologist could come out to the estate to examine me on the morrow. Before he left me, he turned around and added one last thing which caught me off guard.

"Son," he said, quite somberly, "you best stop digging around that old well. Some things are better left unearthed."

He left the room then and locked the door behind him, leaving me alone to speculate whether he hadn't known all along more than he let on.

But whatever inkling he may have had of what was beneath us was minuscule compared to what had been revealed to me – of that I was certain.

Night falls as I write this, and the light leaves the world. When I have fulfilled my destiny, I don't know if it will ever return. The sound from beneath reaches me even during the daylight, even as I am confined to my bedchamber, calling to me distantly but doggedly. I notice with a thrill of excitement that the moon is full this night. The world grows dark, and the call becomes louder. I must heed it.

They have locked me in here like some lunatic mental patient, awaiting the input of some so-called expert, but no matter: I have no intention of waiting here. Before they locked me in I managed to stash a length of rope underneath my bed – the very same that was used to pull me from the hole this morning.

The palms of my hands are covered in oozing sores, and every muscle in my body is stiff and aching, but I bear all this patiently. Very soon it will not matter anymore.

They have filled the hole, I know, but no matter: He will lend me all the strength I need to reach the forgotten door.

To my mother and father, if you are the first to read this, I suppose I should apologise for my behaviour of late. I hope this missive answers some of your questions, before the end. Know that I have not acted out of any malice or resentment towards you, or anyone else. I did not choose my fate. An ancient power beyond the understanding or control of man is beginning to stir, and for reasons beyond my comprehension, I have been chosen to play my small part. Destiny has called me, and I must answer.

His heartbeat quickens. The great Dread awakens, and he is hungry – so very hungry. Once the doom is unleashed, I know not what will come of the world of man, but I suspect this spells a horrible end. I suppose I go now to my death – perhaps I am to be His first taste of man's blood and bone after the long slumber. Regardless, the hour is late, and things cannot be otherwise. The time has come. I must put down my pen and meet my fate.

He calls to me. He is stirring, awakening in the deep. I must open the door for Him.

218

Ponderings of The Orb
A discussion of wizardry and alchemical secrets

I bought the first issue of Bizarchives within a few days of its debut. I'm actually not much of a heavy reader. But since lockdowns I've had serious downtime at my job. So I gave Bizarchives a shot. The guys that produce it are based and the art looked cool. I ended up reading the thing over a few shifts. The short stories and nice variety of genres make it really accessible for guys like me. Even some of the genres that aren't really my cup of tea were fun and introduced me to some stuff I didn't think I'd like. I left it at work and some of the guys have gotten into it too. Now we pick up some of the reprints of old pulps and pass them around, especially the ones about weird monsters and mad scientists. I hope it keeps going.

My only suggestion would be that I hope the editors can find a way to come out with more stuff. It's just not enough stories to hold us over for 6 months. If they could find a way to reduce the price and print something monthly we would totally buy a copy every month. Either way, thanks for showing us blue collar guys that reading can be fun.

--Ty from NY

Hey fellas, great work on issue one. When this dropped I was AMPED. I'm a huge fan of WH40K and Conan. I'm also a lifelong tabletop gamer that plays everything from battle tech to call of cthulhu

219

rpg. Some of the world building found in these bite sized stories were impressive and provided awesome inspiration for my gaming sessions. My favorite stories were Atli's Folly, Shot at Redemption and Lex and the Lost Girl. Lex punching that guy at the end was hilarious and had total antihero energy. MORE LEX!

--Paul

When I think of pulp, I don't necessarily think of sophisticated literature. And although bizarchives has its fair share of zaniness you'd expect from a pulp publication, it also has authors flashing their poetic prowess. Red Ivy and Contest Between Life and Death really showed that short form speculative fiction can also be beautiful. Usually when you pick up something nowadays calling itself "pulp" you get unreadable tryhard irony or hollow crap. Bizarchives managed to hit the warm spot with a mixture of both weirdness and polish. I'm very excited to have caught wind of this project in its infancy so I can watch it blossom.

--Arkham Egg N Cheese

This is just a general comment but the whole ideal behind Bizarchives is a gem and a breath of relief in this age of rubble and ruin.

It gives our Folk a creative outlet and damn are they creative! Once my children are older this will be available to them in my library. Keep going and never stop!

--Dwarf Lord

I'm just an Orbinary guy. They call me Orbille Redenbacher.

--Orb Lord

This is so fun! I love this little community around this book. I lurk in the chats and like to check in and see what the boys are talking about. Dave and company should be very proud of what they're building here. My husband and I read the stories together and discuss the endings. He likes the fantasy stories.I loved Baby Teeth it was so freaky!

One of your authors should try a weird romance story. Maybe not in Bizarchives but in a novelette or something? The stuff they put out for

220

ladies nowadays stinks!

--Dawn LaRose

Grandma moves in was probably the most unsettling story for me. Imagine what corporations would do with our bodies for profit if they could swap consciousnesses. Send us to war or degenerate stuff. I read a lot of SF and keep an eye on transhumanism developments. I haven't seen this concept before in fiction. Pretty chilling...

--McGrinnist

Once you guys get going you should launch a second publication that focuses on war stories, westerns and noirs. Just like the original pulps. I would definitely write a story for it if I wasn't so retarded.

-- Glark Soupermen

I was given a sneak peak at BZA2 because I'm in personal correspondence with the guys. I read Dunelord's Dreaming and the two Lex stories. Dunelord is a short story masterpiece. The plot was succinct, the characters are unique and the world building was stitched in perfectly without distracting from the pace. Undead mercenaries in search for psychedelic pollon to remember their past lives? Just genius.

Both of the Lex stories are heavy contenders too. Bernwick (clever name) despite being a very traditional adventure rescue kind of story was rather exciting. Escape from the cave with the spider things chasing him felt like an action movie. And Odd Village was accurately named. Probably one of the weirdest fantasy shorts I've read. The conversation with the mindsoul at the end had a lot of philosophical implications. I expected Martel to have some writing ability because he's a talented guy but he really surprised me.

If the rest of this second issue are even in the same time zone as these three stories it's going to be very well received.

--anonymous

There was an episode of Bizarcast where Dave was talking with a fellow named Dimes. They brought up a really interesting point. How entities, beings and even certain fantasy races are so humanized. Not in that they're necessarily made into sympathetic characters (they are). But that they're lazily depicted as having common human thoughts and feelings. It really helped me understand Tolkien's elves and how they're perceived. That no matter how much they interact with one another, the two races can never truly understand one another. The sheer fact that elves live for centuries would shape their relationship with their own mortality.

Then it got me wondering how much of our behavior and how we express ourselves is shaped by our lifespans. It seems that newer authors completely overlook these kinds of deep world building. Changing someone's relationship with their mortality could affect everything from language to material culture. Really fascinating concept.

--Hoosierborean

Author Bios

Robert C. Booth
"The Crypt of St. Peter's Church"

Fiction writer who lives in the wooded shade of England's Spine. He has a fascination with the fey and an obsession with the otherworldly. Watch this space for more Reuben Bennet in the near future.

MS Jones
"The Dune Lord's Dreaming"

Subscribe and read more for free at https://illuminatus. substack.com/ or buy from Amazon https://www.amazon.com/ Marcus-S-Jones/e/B01GQ5HQ4U

William "Zac" Gable
"Grim and Serpent"

> A Jack of all trades, and master of some, Zac lives with his wife and children on a small off grid homestead in the Sierra Nevada Mountains of Northern California. He has been a soldier, carpenter, factory worker, mechanic and even a teacher. Now he splits his time between farming, blacksmithing, making jewelry, volunteering as a firefighter and now writing fantasy fiction. Look for his work in future additions of the Bizarchives.

Aaron Robert Geisen
"There Ain't No Pleasing You"

> A cheerful doomsayer, Aaron spends his time lamenting the world-that-was, while begrudgingly walking a straight and narrow path. He finds the macabre funny to such an extent that he considers the story that he submitted to this edition of the Bizarchives to be an out-and-out comedy.

C.J. Miller
"The Sound from Beneath"

> A blue-collar worker, translator, and author from Alberta, the boiler room of Canada. Find his past and future projects at Antelope Hill Publishing.

Emre B. Tan
"To Play The Hero"

> Amateur writer and poet.
> Telegram t.me/CHGAAAA

Froskaz

"The Statement of Carter Brinton"

An aspiring Gothic gentleman, hungry to find ancient texts in old bookshops and ready to sack Rome if need arises. He believes in madness as a political philosophy, and wishes to explore the aesthetics of it in his writings.

A. Cuthbertson

"Crypt of Carnonwe", Co-Editor of *The Bizarchives*: Issue #2

The entity which currently wears the skin of "A. Cuthbertson" is little more than a malevolent presence, making itself felt from across the sea. It seeks to grow its influence, in your lands and in its own, and thanks you for directing your mental energy toward its cause.

Gregory Kay

"Avenger of Oil"

Also author of The Third Revolution and Dark County series, along with the novels *Red Creek Waltz*, *Wings in Darkness*, and *The Barnacles of Ægir*. Originally from West Virginia, living in Florida. Books available on Amazon.

Credits

Dave Martel
Editor-in-Chief
"Lex and the Odd Village", "Lex and the Horror of Benwick Hollows"

- host of "THE BOG" on YouTube, channel: DaveMartel
- project manager for The Epicist magazine (Norroena.org)
- creator of Grimeorth Roleplaying game (Amazon)
- Telegram & Twitter: @TheBoglord

Cyprus Walter
Lead Editor and Book Layout

- The Midgard Institute: themidgardinstitute.wordpress.com
- Midgard Poetry: midgardpoetry.wordpress.com

Donald Kent
Cover Art & Layout

- AmericanZarathustra.com

Michael Sagginario
Book Layout

- Irminfolk Odinist Community: Irminfolk.com

Arbogast
Co-Editor

- writer, editor, blogger: 1325publishing.blogspot.com
- author of "Nocturnes," a volume of poetry.

For more publications, info about the pulp genre, and much more, visit our website:

thebizarchives.com

for live updates & announcements,
follow us on
Telegram & Twitter:

@theBizArchives

The Enchanted Wall

Immortalized here are the names of The Bizarchives' most illustrious denizens. Due to their contributions we as a weird fiction publication are able to pursue our path into the horizons of destiny:

Sarah Dye

Faysik Tedsson

Big Hair Tsunami

Made in the USA
Coppell, TX
10 October 2022

84339098R00136